✳ ✳ ✳

Everyone has heard the story—the dwarves,
the talking mirror, the evil witch. But this tale
doesn't belong to Snow White anymore. . . .

P. W. CATANESE'S
FURTHER TALES ADVENTURES:

THE EYE OF THE WARLOCK

✳

THE BRAVE APPRENTICE

✳

THE THIEF AND THE BEANSTALK

The Mirror's Tale

A FURTHER TALES ADVENTURE

P. W. CATANESE

ALADDIN PAPERBACKS
NEW YORK   LONDON   TORONTO   SYDNEY

The Mirror's Tale

This book is a work of fiction. Any references to historical events,
real people, or real locales are used fictitiously.
Other names, characters, places, and incidents are the product
of the author's imagination, and any resemblance to actual events or locales
or persons, living or dead, is entirely coincidental.

ALADDIN PAPERBACKS
An imprint of Simon & Schuster Children's Publishing Division
1230 Avenue of the Americas, New York, NY 10020
Text copyright © 2006 by P. W. Catanese
All rights reserved, including the right of reproduction
in whole or in part in any form.
ALADDIN PAPERBACKS and colophon
are trademarks of Simon & Schuster, Inc.
Designed by Karin Paprocki
The text of this book was set in Adobe Jenson.
Manufactured in the United States of America
First Aladdin Paperbacks edition June 2006
4 6 8 10 9 7 5
Library of Congress Control Number 2005938723
ISBN-13: 978-1-4169-1251-4 — ISBN-10: 1-4169-1251-7

※　✳　✳

For Joe and Cathy Stenza

✳ ✳ ✳

With four novels in the rearview mirror, I'd like to thank some of the people who've been essential to their creation. My editor, Molly McGuire, for her wonderful instincts and for being a pleasure to work with. My agent, Peter Rubie, for pulling my first manuscript from a sea of submissions and giving an unpublished author a chance. My wife, Lisa, for her love, encouragement, support, and keen eye. My children, Kristina, Michael, and Andrew, for devouring my books as fast as I can print them and being the first to catch mistakes. And the friends who've been kind enough to read and respond to my early drafts. I'd also like to express my particular gratitude to the teachers who've read my books aloud in class. You guys are the best.

✳

"It was just a trick," Bert offered. Beside him, his brother nodded vigorously.

"Just a trick!" Baron Charmaigne roared. He swung the fire poker and smashed the burning logs. A thousand sparks flew up and winked out, and a handful of orange embers rolled out of the hearth and onto the stone floor of the great hall. The baron crushed them under his boot.

Bert stole a glance at Will, who stared at their father with widening eyes while his fingernails dug into his knees.

"Let's talk about this *trick* of yours," Baron Charmaigne said, stabbing the air with the poker. "Margaret! Do you know what they did?"

"No, my lord," Margaret said quietly. Besides the baron and his sons, the old servant was the only one in the room. She stood with her wrinkled hands clasped and her gaze fixed on the fireplace.

"Of course you don't. That's part of the problem, isn't it? Well, let me tell you. The victim *this* time was a gullible farm girl whose family just moved to the village.

Apparently as she was shooing birds from the seeded fields, a boy carrying a large basket approached and offered to show her 'a fine surprise.' The girl described him as 'a pale but handsome lad with wide, blue eyes and a wild, black mane.'"

Bert reached up to smooth his unkempt hair, then checked his laughter as he noticed Will doing the same. It wouldn't be wise to laugh at this moment.

"This black-haired villain then sat and covered himself with the basket," the baron said. He put his back to the others and spoke into the flames. "A moment later, the girl said, there was a tap on her shoulder. To her everlasting horror the boy now stood *behind* her. The same pale, blue-eyed boy in the same clothes, she said. Then he walked to the basket and turned it over to reveal its emptiness. And, of course, she ran off screaming, sending the entire village into an uproar." The baron turned to face the boys again. His face had gone purple with rage.

"It was us, Father," said Will, looking paler than usual, if that was possible. He appeared to be shrinking.

"I bloody well know it was the two of you!"

Bert sat up straight and cleared his throat. "I crept out from the basket and hid when she turned around to look at Will."

"But we didn't expect her to run off screaming about witches and the devil," Will said to the floor.

The baron gritted his teeth and pressed his palms against his temples. "I'm doubly angry!" he cried. "Angry once because this is more of the foolishness, the horrid behavior that your mother and I have scolded you for from the moment you monsters reared up on two legs. And angry again because you've stirred up all the fears we've tried to put to rest. Half these peasants still believe those ridiculous stories about the Witch-Queen!"

"But Margaret says they're true—" Bert cut himself off, instantly regretting the words. Margaret seemed to wilt as the baron's anger turned toward her like the door of a furnace swinging open.

"Margaret. We've asked you to watch the twins. To help shape them. To do something about their behavior, for heaven's sake. But instead you fill their heads with these foolish stories." The baron paused to think. He sounded weary when he spoke again. "We've given you a dozen years with them, Margaret, but they are falling far short of my expectations. Your service here is over. I want you to leave Ambercrest. By tomorrow."

"Father, no!" the boys said as one. Bert tried to leap off the bench, but Will grabbed his sleeve and held him down.

Margaret could have said so many things at that moment to deflect the baron's anger back toward the boys, to help him understand that they simply refused to be tamed. But she only whispered, "Yes, my lord. It has been my honor to serve you," and quietly left the room.

"It's wrong," said Bert, pacing back and forth across the floor of Margaret's tiny room.

"It's completely unfair," said Will. He sat with his back against the wall and bounced his head gently against the stone.

"I won't be alone. I have a niece who serves at a manor not far from here, and I can stay with her." Margaret was packing her frocks and aprons with a few other modest possessions into a small chest.

"Here, Margaret. We want you to have this." Bert tugged a thick-banded ring of gold off his finger and held it out to her.

Margaret's eyebrows rose and fell. "I cannot possibly accept that."

"I wish you'd take it," said Bert. "It's my fault you're being sent away. Because of what I said. It is true, though, isn't it? About the Witch-Queen and Snow White?"

"There is some truth in it, for sure. And my grandmother heard the story from the princess herself before she died. She told me that even as an old woman you could look at Emelina—the one they called Snow White—and know that she was fair beyond description." Margaret smiled at the twins. "There's plenty of Snow White in the two of you, that's plain to see, even after so many generations. That skin, those eyes . . ." She sighed and closed the lid on the chest. "Young men, I'm afraid your parents will do something far more drastic if you disobey them again. Promise me you'll try to be good."

"I promise," Will said quietly.

Bert grunted. "When I'm baron, the first order I give will be to bring you back."

"I didn't know your father had named his successor," Margaret said, looking from Bert to Will.

"It'll probably be me," said Bert. "Will doesn't even want the barony. That's what he always says. Right, Will?"

"I guess," Will said to the floor. His face reddened.

"Now, Bert, don't underestimate your brother," Margaret said. "He's got a good heart and a lot of wisdom in that head. But no matter what happens, the most important thing is for the two of you to stay friends."

"Of course we will!" said Bert. Will nodded.

"Well, I don't know which of you will grow up to be baron," Margaret said, "but I'll try to live long enough to see that day. Until then, good-bye." The twins hugged her. A servant came in and carried the chest away, and then Margaret was gone.

"I wish she'd taken the ring," said Will.

"I stuck it in the chest when she wasn't looking," said Bert.

CHAPTER
2

Margaret rode in the wagon that the baron's courier, Parley—dear, kind, funny Parley, who had somehow managed to make her smile even on this terrible day—had arranged for her. She took a final look at Ambercrest. As the road bent around the forest, a green curtain was drawn across the castle that had been her home for so many years.

The lines in her face deepened as she thought back to the cold, winter night she saw the omen.

It was thirteen years ago on a night as dark and cold as a crypt. She remembered how she shivered in her bed, and then heard someone awake in the inky halls of Ambercrest, hours before sunrise. Not the stomping boots of a guard, but the silky shuffle of slippers. A pale, orange light appeared in the slender space at the bottom of her door. She was already there with a hand on the knob when the rapping began.

It was the baroness. "Margaret, I am with child," she said. "I'm certain of it now."

"Wonderful news, my lady. The baron will be pleased." Margaret noticed that even at this late hour, with no one about, the baroness had taken a moment to compose her hair.

"Yes," the baroness said uncertainly. "They say a woman's face glows with beauty when she is with child. Let us hope that is true."

There was a soundless interlude, and Margaret worked her jaw sideways and pressed her gums together to suppress a yawn. "May I be of service to you, my lady?"

"Of course. I must have something to eat. And it must be . . . eggs. That's what the child wants, I feel."

"Right away, Baroness."

With a lamp to light her way, Margaret went down the wide stone staircase, through the great hall and the dining room, and out the door of the keep into the bitter cold. The short walk across the courtyard and into the kitchen tower sent needles of pain into her joints.

"No sense waking the cook for this, I can manage it," she muttered. The eggs were kept in a wooden bowl on a shelf. Only one was left, but it was a goose egg and quite large. She picked it up, but her fingers were still numb from the frigid air. The egg slipped from her grasp and broke with a splat on the stone floor.

Margaret sighed. She knelt to see if enough of the egg could be preserved. Holding the lamp close by, she stared at it for a long while, wondering. She shivered again, but not from the cold this time.

Spilled from the single shell were two yolks, like golden islands in a clear sea. *This can only mean one thing*, she thought. But then her smile settled into a thin frown.

One yolk remained whole, but the other had not survived the fall. Its fine skin had split, and the inner yolk oozed out, slowly and shapelessly.

Bert sat on the stone sill of the window and dangled one leg outside. He had a disk of polished tin in one hand and was staring at his reflection, searching for any sign of whiskers on his narrow chin. It struck him that looking in the little mirror was just like looking at his brother. "You know," he said, "I might be Will and you might be Bert."

"What do you mean?" Will asked. He was lying on his bed, propped on his elbows.

"Don't you remember? Mother and Father could never tell us apart. They still can't. They kept a ribbon tied around my ankle—or *your* ankle—when we were babies. But, remember, Margaret said she once found us both playing with the ribbon that I had untied. Or that *you* untied. So we may not be who we think we are. Either one of us could be firstborn, so either one of us could be baron."

"I'm sure it'll be you, Bert."

Bert couldn't suppress a smile. "That'll be up to Father. But I wouldn't mind— Hey, what's going on out there?" He peered down into the courtyard. One of the

9

baron's men had thundered through the gates on horse-back. He thrust the reins into a stable boy's hands and strode toward the great hall, nearly breaking into a run. "It's Edward, the smelly one. Something urgent, I don't know what. Should we find out?"

Will didn't say a word. He just sprang from his bed and followed Bert out the door. Soon they were at the balcony overlooking the great hall, where their father had already received Edward. The boys lay fl at on the fl oor with their heads raised just high enough for spy-ing, and strained to hear the conversation.

"I can hardly believe it," the baron said. "After so many years. There is no doubt it was them? Not simply poachers or some band of ruffians?"

"Please understand that I did not witness it with my own eyes, sire. But John did. Although it was from a distance, he is certain. They were gone by the time we rode up. No trace of them at all."

"They can do that. Disappear on you just like that." Baron Charmaigne snapped his fingers. "Well, I want those hills searched, every rock turned over, every crevice explored. If they've come back, I'll have their heads, I promise you that. Come, I want to talk to John myself." Edward followed the baron out of the room, but neither said anything the boys could hear. Bert and Will looked at each other and shrugged.

* * *

Will awoke that night, flailing under his blanket. Something was pinching his nostrils closed. His eyes focused on Bert, grinning down at him.

"What's the matter with you?" Will said after he swatted Bert's hand away.

"Do you know how hard it is to wake you up?"

"I couldn't sleep at all for a while," Will muttered. "I kept thinking about Margaret. What did you get me up for, anyway?"

"I think I know what Father and Smelly Ed were talking about."

Will ground his knuckles into his eyes. "Can't you tell me tomorrow?"

"This is too good to wait! Come on," Bert said. He led the way to the door, eased it open, and crept out into the dark hallway. Will took up his usual position a few steps behind. They moved with practiced stealth past the room where their mother and father slept, and padded down the wide, curving stairs to the great hall. A tall candle burned at the foot of the steps. Bert produced a smaller candle and holder from his pocket and held its wick to the flame. "We need to see the maps," he whispered to Will.

They crossed the main hall and passed through a slender archway into the small, musty chamber where the baron kept his maps. A broad table stood against the back wall. Above it were ten rows of pigeonholes, filled with rolled parchments that stuck out above the table. "Here, I think it's this one," said Bert. He pulled out the longest parchment. Dust floated gently down, tiny bits of matter illuminated by the light of the candle.

Bert spread his arms wide to unroll the big map, shoving the candle to the rear of the table to make room. There were smooth river stones on the table to keep the parchments from curling. He placed one on each corner of the map.

"We shouldn't be here. We're already in trouble," Will said.

"Too late! We're here. So, you know what Father's chief responsibility is, right?"

Will yawned. "I'm too tired to remember."

Bert let out an exaggerated sigh. "Come on, Will. You know full well; you're the one who pokes his nose into the archives all the time. Ambercrest is one of the most remote castles in the kingdom—only The Crags is farther north, and nobody cares about that place. Father is supposed to keep watch on the borders for our enemies. *These* borders." Bert tapped his finger on the parchment.

The map showed the northern reaches of the king's realm. Bert's finger drummed on the mountains just north of Ambercrest and The Crags, mountains labeled with a phrase that Will read aloud: "The realm of the Dwergh."

"That's right, the Dwergh. I think that's what the patrol saw out there, somewhere between here and The

Crags. Remember what Smelly Ed said to Father, that whoever it was just disappeared? That's what those filthy little Dwergh do—they crawl into their holes where you can't find them. Like moles."

"How do you know they're filthy?" Will asked. "You've never seen one."

"I've heard stories, Will. They're grubby, greedy monsters. They're strong, but they're short—shorter than you and me, even. They'll kill you for the gold on your fingers. I heard they steal babies and eat them. And do you know what they do to prisoners? It's too horrible to describe."

"Really?" Will said, looking with dread at the peaks on the map. "But . . . they're not all like that, right? What about the ones that helped our great-great-grandmother? Or whatever she was."

"Two more greats, I think. Listen, Will, those Dwergh might have saved her from the Witch-Queen. But they didn't do it for *her*, they did it for themselves. They probably made her promise to give them all the jewels at The Crags in exchange for protecting her."

"I never thought of it that way," Will said. He rubbed the back of his head. "Do you really think the Dwergh are back?"

"I hope so. It's so boring around here, guarding a border when the enemy's been hiding inside mountains for fifty years. Why wait? We should just go after them. What a fight that would be!"

"Bert, don't you ever read the stuff I show you? You can't just march into their mountains. It's bad strategy. First off, they've already got the high ground. And how are you going to supply your army? You can't even—"

"Oh please," Bert interrupted, waving his hand. "You and those translations. It's stupid, all that stuff about strategies and deception. You have to charge right at them, that's what Father would do." Bert frowned, wondering why the map was suddenly so much easier to read. A flickering orange glow had flooded the room. Will gasped, and Bert's head jerked up, and his eyes nearly burst from their sockets.

The candle that Bert pushed to the back of the table had ignited the map just above it, and the flames leaped eagerly to the other parchments.

"Let's get out of here!" cried Bert.

"No, we have to put it out!" Will said.

"What? Right!" said Bert. He pulled the candle away from the pigeonholes and swatted at the flames with his open palm. "Ouch!" Bits of burning paper floated about, and a few more maps began to smolder. A dense cloud of smoke gathered in the chamber's rounded ceiling. "Will, get the water bucket by the hearth!"

Will's grimace nearly stretched from one ear to the other as he ran into the great hall, where the day's fire had settled into a sputtering gray heap. He lifted the iron bucket with a grunt and waddled awkwardly back to the chamber with the pail swinging between his legs. By the time he got back, Bert had stripped off his nightshirt and was batting the flaming ends of the parchments. "Put the bucket on the table!" he said, trying not to shout.

Bert grabbed the parchments and stuck the burning ends into the bucket, where they hissed like snakes. When the last of the maps had been extinguished, he and Will crammed them back into the holes. They stepped back and looked at the result. Soggy, blackened parchments stuck out at all angles with a third of their lengths burned away by the fire. Will shook his head and groaned. "Maybe they won't notice."

"Right. *Now* let's get out of here," Bert said, picking up his charred nightshirt. "You'd better put the bucket back."

Will lifted the pail. When he turned and saw Edward blocking the archway and staring at them, he dropped it again. The bucket tipped over, and the water sloshed out into a puddle that engulfed Edward's feet.

The boys froze. Edward sniffed the air and looked at the cloud of smoke still trapped overhead. His eyebrows rose as he glanced at the ruined maps, and then at Bert standing naked with a strand of smoke still drifting up from the nightshirt he held bunched against his waist.

"We didn't do it," Bert ventured.

Edward snorted.

"You won't tell, will you?" Will asked in a strangled voice.

"Let's see," Edward said. "I could say nothing, then have your father use me for an archery target when he finds out I lied. Or I could say something, and you two ruffians could get what you deserve. Dear me, what should I do?"

Will closed his eyes and shivered, thinking about the look on his mother's face when Edward led her to the map chamber. When she ordered them to their room, it was with a colder fury than he'd ever seen before. Starting that fire wasn't the worst thing they'd ever done, but something about her expression told Will they'd made one mistake too many. "What do you think they're going to do?"

"Dunno. Maybe Father will have us beheaded," Bert replied. He was at the window, staring into the black sky. "Hush for a minute," he said. He stuck his head out and cocked his ear toward the left. Will got out of bed and leaned out with him. Their parents were talking in the room next door, and their voices were rising.

"Can't quite hear what they're saying," Will said. "Doesn't sound promising, though."

"It doesn't," Bert agreed. "I wish they didn't lock us in. Otherwise we could just sneak out and listen at their door." His expression brightened. He ran to his bed, reached underneath it, and pulled out a coiled rope from the clutter of objects that was crammed into the narrow space.

"Bert, I don't think that's a good—"

"They're talking about us!" Bert said. "Don't you want to know what the punishment will be?" He knotted one end of the rope around his waist and threw the rest of the coil to his brother. "Tie this end to something, in case I slip. Although death might be better than what they're planning."

"You're crazy," Will said wearily. He knelt to tie the rope to the foot of his bed.

"Not crazy," Bert replied, grinning. "Just terribly brave." He stuck his legs out the window and lowered himself on his stomach until his elbows rested on the sill. He probed with his toes until he found a narrow ledge of stone, an inch or so wide, that ran just below the second story of the castle. He and Will had spent countless hours edging their way along the walls of the keep—but always on the first floor, where a slip would only send them a few feet to the ground. Here, the courtyard was at least twenty feet below. Bert didn't see any of the night watchmen down there. And that was good. To them he would look like an assassin creeping toward the baron's room.

He edged away from the window, looked for tiny cracks between the stones that he could use as fingerholds, and slid his feet along the ledge, an inch at a time.

Will watched his slow progress and fed the rope out, ready to hold on tight if his brother lost his balance.

By the time Bert was halfway to his parent's window, he could hear their conversation clearly.

"They'll never change, you know," his mother said.

"Hellions, both of them," his father replied. "And punishment only makes them more rebellious."

"But why do they do this, Walter? It's almost as if they are *trying* to upset me. To get back at me for something."

"But what have you . . . what have *we* ever done to them to deserve all this?"

"Nothing, I'm sure. But they're wild and unruly, and something must be done. What if they'd burned themselves to death? What would the king's court say about us then?"

Thanks, Mother, Bert thought. There was a long silence that was somehow worse than their words. He managed to creep to the very edge of the window before his mother spoke again, much more softly.

"Walter, do you remember the story of your grandfather's assault on the Northmen? How he won the day?"

"Of course," said the baron. He sounded relieved to change the topic. "The armies faced each other across a wide plain. Grandfather concentrated his forces on the center of the Northmen's line and attacked there, splitting the army into two."

"Just so."

There was another long silence. Somewhere in the dark courtyard below, a dog growled. It occurred to Bert that the topic had not changed at all. Inside the room the same thing occurred to his father.

"You think we should separate the boys."

"Yes! Send one to live with your brother at The Crags. Not forever, only for the summer. And keep one with us. It may be the only way to tame them."

No, Bert thought. His brain faltered, and his knees went limp. He tightened his grip on the edge of the windowsill and turned to look back at Will, who leaned out the window with a puzzled look on his face.

"Separate the boys," the baron said again, as if he was trying to get used to the idea.

"They lead each other into trouble. Bertram leads William into trouble, to be more exact."

"But they've always been together. From the day they were born. I can hardly remember seeing one without the other."

"That's the problem, don't you see?" she said. Bert leaned closer. His parents were so close to the window that he could hear the rustle of fabric as his mother drew nearer to his father. Bert could picture what was happening inside. He'd seen it before. When his mother really wanted his father to agree to something, she'd slide up beside him and lock her hands around his waist. "It will be a shock, but a shock is what they need," she said. "Honestly, Walter, there have been times when

I wonder if I even love them, they are so troublesome. I know you feel the same way, you don't even have to say it. We must do something. You need to name your successor before long, and how can you even choose between them now? One's a monster, the other's a . . . a *mouse*."

There was another pause, the longest yet. Bert realized that he was trembling, down to the tips of his fingers and toes. He squeezed his eyes shut. *Don't do it, Father*, he thought. *Don't listen to her. We'll be good, I promise. I'll stop getting Will into trouble, I swear it.*

His father's voice again drifted out into the night. "Which would we send?"

"Will, I suppose," his mother said. "He won't misbehave and embarrass us the way Bert would. Will's clever enough, but he's as meek as a lamb without his brother to follow."

Bert swallowed hard and felt a lump in his throat the size of a paving stone. He looked back toward Will, who couldn't hear any of this. His brother waved his hand in a mad circle, urging him to come back. But Bert couldn't go yet. He had to hear what his father would say. Send Will to The Crags? They couldn't—didn't they know how scared Will got whenever he left the castle grounds? Bert leaned even closer to the window. *Father, please . . .*

"No," his father said at last. Bert let out a long, grateful sigh. His mother began to protest, but his father cut her off. "But that was the last act of foolishness I will tolerate. Tomorrow I'll tell them they have one final chance. And if they misstep one more time, I will do exactly what you propose."

A wide smile flowered on Bert's face, and he straightened up, ready to return to his room. He was dizzy with relief. *That was a near miss,* he thought. *Will's going to faint when he finds out.* For a moment their world had been like a crystal bowl teetering on the edge of a shelf, about to shatter into a million pieces. It seemed safe once more until a harsh voice called out from below.

"You there! What are you up to?"

It was a watchman in the courtyard. Bert's chest was against the wall, and he twisted his torso to look down at the fellow, hoping the man would shut up once he saw it was only the baron's son. He tapped his forefinger against his lips. And then his father's head popped out of the window, like a jack-in-the-box, just a foot from his face.

The baron screamed. Bert yelped, and the fingers of his other hand slipped out of the crack that he was holding onto. His father tried to grab Bert's arm as he toppled away from the wall, but only caught Bert's sleeve, which tore and slipped through his fingers. Bert looked with wild eyes toward his brother who gritted his teeth and tightly gripped the rope in his fists. Bert fell, and when the rope went taut between them, Will was tugged neatly out the window as if he was diving into a pond. Bert tried to scream again, but said only "*Ooof!*" as the knot around his waist bit into his stomach. He swung like a pendulum toward a point somewhere under his own room, bouncing and bumping along the rugged face of the wall. Will held the rope long enough to flip himself upright again, but lost his grip and slid down the cord's length until he straddled Bert's shoulders. Above them Bert could hear Will's bed scrape across the stone floor, and they sank a few more feet until they nearly reached the courtyard, where the watchman approached them with his sword in his hand and a bemused expression on his face.

Bert had the urge to laugh until he heard the furious voice bellow down. "Spying? On your own father? That was the last straw! You hear me? *The very last straw!*"

"It's only for a few months," the baron said, when the wailing quieted to the point where he might be heard.

"No!" the boys shouted. They were standing against a wall when their father broke the news, but in their shock they slid down and hunched on the cold stone floor.

The baron glared at them. "Enough of your insolence. This decision will not be undone. I've sent word ahead to your uncle Hugh that Will is coming."

Bert looked at his brother, who'd gone paler than he thought possible. "But why Will? Why not me?"

"I'll go," Will said. He sounded as if he was about to be sick.

"No!" shouted Bert. He stared at his father with fierce, round eyes. "You can't send Will to that awful place. Don't you know how frightened he gets?"

The baron palmed his forehead and groaned. "Bert. For the last time, there is nothing to fear at The Crags. The stories are nonsense. There are no witches, no beasts. Your uncle and aunt live there, for heaven's sake. And if Will is so easily frightened, why is he never afraid to break my rules?"

"Because I talk him into everything. He's more afraid of me leaving him alone than he is of breaking your stupid rules," Bert said. "Don't you see, I'm the one who causes all the trouble! It was my idea to sneak down to the map chamber, my idea to spy on you and Mother. All the bad ideas are mine—but you never talk to us except to scold us, so you'd never know that!"

The baron opened his mouth to speak, but the words spilled from Bert, like wine from a shattered cask. "And all Mother ever does is tell us we're too disobedient, or too lazy, or too dirty, or we're not fit to be heirs to the barony, because she's just like you and she doesn't really care—"

"Enough!" the baron roared. Bert fell silent. He and Will hung their heads as their father loomed over them. The baron stabbed at the air with a fat finger to punctuate his words. "This decision is *final*. Blame no one but your*selves*. The carriage leaves this afternoon, and *Will* shall be on it." Bert raised his face and stared back defiantly. "And if you say another word," the baron said, almost growling, "I'll have you whipped like a common thief."

The boys climbed the last few steps to the watchtower on the inner wall, a round room of stone with a spire at the top and three windows shaped like narrow, inverted shields. It was deserted, as always. Since the outer wall had been constructed decades before, there was no need for anyone to come here. So it was the perfect place to meet—usually to hide or play or hatch devious plans, but this time to mourn. Will sat on the floor, picking up clay marbles and letting them roll off his hand into the pile of sand. Bert stared out the window at the landscape that surrounded the castle.

Ambercrest sat imperiously on a tall mound of earth. The land sloped away in every direction, so that even though the outer walls were built taller, the inner walls sat higher, and the old watchtower offered a splendid view of the countryside.

Beyond the outer wall the humble cottages and barns made the castle seem that much grander. It was early summer, and the distant forest had bloomed into its full green glory. Roads stretched in four directions, as if the castle itself was the center of a compass. Bert gazed along the northern road: the one that would take away Will. He turned to his brother. Will had his knees tucked against his chest and his arms around his legs. Bert thought he might be trembling.

"It'll be all right," Bert said.

"It won't," Will said. "Bert, you know me. I don't like leaving the castle. When we go past the walls, I can hardly breathe."

"But you and I have snuck out there a couple of times."

"I know—when you're with me, I can just barely manage it. It's as if . . . I don't know. As if you're my courage. Because you've got enough for both of us."

Bert sighed deeply. He sat cross-legged in front of his brother and rested his chin on his cupped hands. It was true about Will; the thought of leaving home always sent him into a panic. Once, when they were very young, their family went to The Crags for the wedding of Uncle Hugh to Lady Elaine. It was one of Bert's oldest memories. Will cried the whole way there. It made their parents turn red with shame. And when they finally arrived at that grim, foreboding place in the shadow of the mountains, Will's histrionics only grew worse.

"I wish it was me they were sending," Bert said. "I wouldn't mind seeing The Crags again. That's even closer to the Dwergh. Maybe Uncle Hugh would let me go out on the patrols. If there's a fight with those tunnel rats, it'll start there."

Will had tucked his face between his knees. Bert heard him sniffing. He rolled his eyes. His brother was his best friend, but he could be a baby at times. How could his father even think of sending Will to The Crags?

"It should be me that goes," Bert said. *Wait*, he thought. "It *can* be me."

"What are you talking about?" Will's head rose. He rubbed a sleeve under his nose.

Bert chuckled. He was smiling again. "It's so obvious! I'll go in your place. It'll be easy to fool them; they can hardly tell us apart as it is! Here's what we're going to do. . . ."

"Good-bye, Bert," said Bert.

"Good-bye, Will," replied Will.

They'd said their real farewell an hour before. This one was just for show. They hugged and thumped each other on the back.

"You'll write to me, won't you?" whispered Will. "Parley says he'll be going to The Crags soon."

"I'll write, and so will you," said Bert into his brother's ear. He straightened up, winked at Will, and walked over to the carriage where his father and mother waited. It was a small carriage with broad wheels, drawn by a pair of horses. Four people could have fit inside, but the only passenger for this journey would be him.

The driver, Matthias, was occupied with the reins. A

small escort of four mounted soldiers waited nearby. Their horses tossed their heads and pawed at the ground.

"We thought you'd prefer the carriage, Will," his mother said. Her voice was as flat as the castle pond on a windless day. "I'm sure Bert would have insisted on riding a horse if it was him that was going."

You've got that right, Bert thought, suppressing a smirk. "Of course, Mother. Thank you," he said with all the meekness he could manage. "I'm sorry about what happened. About everything."

"You can prove that you're sorry by behaving yourself at The Crags," his mother said.

"Exactly," the baron said, opening the carriage door. "In you go, Will."

Bert stared at the ground and let his shoulders slump, doing his best impression of his brother. His parents were fooled completely. It made him feel triumphant and sad at the same time. *How can this be so easy?*

The door closed. His mother walked away, and a moment later his father's head poked in through the window in the carriage door. "Will, before you go . . . I realize this won't be easy for you. I know it scares you to leave home."

Bert forced his bottom lip to tremble and pretended to wipe a tear from the inner corner of his eye. "I'll do my best, Father," he said.

"I'm happy to hear it." The baron frowned at the driver. "Matthias, give us a moment," he called up.

"Yes, my lord," the driver said. He hopped down from his seat and wandered over to talk to the escorts.

The baron leaned even farther into the carriage. Bert sensed that he was about to hear something important.

"Will . . . There are two things I need to tell you before you go. First, I have a mission for you."

"A mission?" Bert asked. He had to fight to keep his enthusiasm in check. "What kind of mission?" he said, letting his voice crack.

"I want you to keep an eye on your uncle Hugh. I've gotten the sense that he might be up to something at The Crags."

"Up to what, Father?"

"You must know that Hugh has always been jealous of me, how the king favors me, and how I became baron instead of him—even though he's the older brother. And he was furious when I ordered him to occupy The Crags as an outpost. He considered it a kind of exile. I sometimes fear that he may be trying to set up his own little kingdom up there."

"Really?" Bert's heart pounded, and his legs bounced on the seat. This was the most exciting thing he'd ever heard.

"Keep your voice down, Will. And don't be afraid. There's probably nothing to it—I wouldn't let you go if I thought it was real. But I still want you to observe.

Count how many soldiers your uncle has—it shouldn't be more than eighty. See if he's stockpiling weapons or horses. Just watch, that's all. I don't want you to do anything stupid or rash—if I wanted that, I would have sent your brother."

Bert winced and sank back into his seat. "I'm sure Bert would have done a good job."

The baron shook his head. "Your brother's too reckless. He never thinks, he just acts, and never worries about the consequences. I'm not ignorant, Will—I know which one of you causes all the trouble. And that brings me to the second thing."

Bert put a hand on his stomach. Suddenly he didn't feel well. His words came out thick and slurred. "What is it, Father?"

The baron spoke even more quietly this time. Bert could see a thin smile through his sparce, black beard. His father's eyes twinkled. "I know everyone believes that Bert will be baron one day. But I wouldn't assume that if I were you."

Bert's mouth dropped open. He felt like a cold dagger had been thrust into his gut.

His father winked. He must have figured the surprise was a pleasant one. "Being a baron isn't about running around with a sword, looking for fights. A strong brain is just as important as a strong arm. And I know you're the wiser of the two. Smarter, and more sensible."

Now the dagger was being twisted.

"But . . . Father . . ." Bert sputtered weakly. If he spoke too loud, he thought he might throw up.

"Nothing's decided yet, Will, so don't go off thinking the barony is yours just yet. But consider this as a test. If you handle yourself well . . . if you can find your courage out there at The Crags . . . you know what I mean." The baron offered an encouraging, toothy grin.

"Of course," Bert said quietly.

"That's my Will," said the baron, clapping Bert on the shoulder. He turned to shout. "Ready, Matthias!"

W ill dashed around the back of the keep as soon as the carriage left. He ran to a corner of the inner wall and into the dark doorway that led to the stairs. Bert and he would always race to the top, and Bert would always win. Will felt a pinch in his heart, keenly aware of his brother's absence.

He bounded up—three steps at a time until his legs weakened, then two steps, then one, until he finally arrived in the neglected watchtower. His chest heaved as he gasped for air, openmouthed. He leaned out the window and peered out, shielding his eyes from the sun.

The carriage had just passed through the gate of the outer wall. Will waited for Bert to lean out the window of the carriage. "Go to the tower," Bert had whispered just before they stepped outside to act out their goodbye. "I'll wave one last time before I'm out of sight. Be sure to wave back."

Will watched as the carriage rolled down the dusty road, approaching the forest that would hide it from sight. Four horsemen formed the corners of a square around it. Will held his hand halfway up, ready to wave, and wondered if Bert had forgotten. Finally, before the carriage disappeared, Will raised his arm and swept it back and forth, hoping his brother might at least peek out and see it.

Bert was gone. A breeze whistled through the tower. Will felt a strange and foreign sensation creep across him. It made him sink to his knees and put his forehead on the cold stone floor of the watchtower.

He was alone.

CHAPTER

5

Bert sat quietly for the first hour of the trip, letting every bump in the road jostle him from side to side. He'd replaced the gold ring he'd given to Margaret with an iron band, which bore the family crest, and he twisted it back and forth around his finger until the skin was sore. A hot, sour taste bubbled up his throat. He took a long sip from one of the skins of water that had been packed for him. When he was done, he hurled it onto the facing seat. His mouth puckered and trembled, and his eyes felt hot and wet. "No," he muttered. "I won't cry." He pummeled the sides of the carriage, stomped his feet, and hissed through his bared teeth.

A face appeared to his right. It was one of the soldiers, leaning down from his horse to peer in through the open window in the door. "Are you having a fit in there?" the soldier said.

Bert stared coldly at the fellow. "Am I *what?*"

The soldier cleared his throat. "Pardon me, Master Will. Your father said I should keep an eye on you. In case you have a fit of hysteria . . . You know, what with you being afraid to leave home . . ."

Bert's lip twitched on one side. "Don't worry about me. Just watch the woods for those Dwergh." He folded his arms and glared out the other window.

"Riight," he heard the soldier say, stretching the sound of the word. The noise of hooves faded a bit. Bert heard the soldier mutter something to one of the other escorts. They snickered, thinking they were too quiet for him to hear.

I hear you, all right, Bert thought.

On the first day, the road passed through meadows and fields, and the river beside it ran wide and smooth. The commoners they met scurried off the path and watched respectfully as the carriage rolled by.

They spent the night on the sandy shore at a bend in the river. Bert lay awake for hours while some of the escorts snored away and two kept watch at the edge of the circle of orange firelight. His father's parting words were like a song he couldn't get out of his head. A terrible, haunting song.

But Will doesn't even want to be baron. That's what he's always said, Bert thought, with the back of his thumb clamped between his teeth. *Isn't it? Except that day Margaret left. Then he said, "I guess," like he wasn't so sure anymore. . . .*

On the second day, the climbing began, and Bert felt himself leaning relentlessly toward the back of the carriage.

They'd reached the foothills of the mountains and the Cliff Road, so called because it hugged the top of a ledge with a perilous drop into the valley below. To the left the land sloped up into a thick forest of pine.

Bert nearly tumbled off his seat as the carriage stopped abruptly. He heard Matthias shout, and he leaned out the window to learn the cause. The driver stood, pointing into the trees, and two of the horsemen charged off in that direction. Bert heard the horses clop—left to right and back again—from deep in the woods, and the men call to each other. The riders returned to the carriage, shaking their heads and shrugging. They laughed and mocked Matthias for seeing things that weren't there, and the driver muttered something about the enemies of the baron.

The cliff finally shrank as the floor of the valley rose to meet it. Dark mountains loomed ahead, marking the brink of the barony and the kingdom. Somewhere on the other side of those peaks the Dwergh lived. Bert heard knuckles rap the top of the carriage. Matthias called down from the driver's perch. "You can see The Crags now, Master Will."

Despite his wretched mood Bert felt a thrill fly up his spine. He had only the vaguest memory of the place, from the first time he'd been here. And in truth his brother was not the only one who found it scary. Bert leaned farther out the window, so he could look straight ahead of them. And there it was, not a mile away.

The Crags was less than half the size of Ambercrest, but somehow more daunting. The castle was nestled against the side of the nearest mountain. Its bulging, irregular walls met the steep mountainside at both ends, forming a dark half-circle of stone. The keep inside was perhaps two stories tall with a terrace on top. What a contrast from Bert's home, sitting on its neat, green mound with its graceful towers whitened with lime. It looked like something built by an ancient race, exciting and alive with secrets. Beautiful? Certainly not, but someone tried to make it inviting. He caught a glimpse of flowers on the terrace, and there were pretty shrubs in bloom beside the gate. Colorful flags and pennants flew from its watchtowers, twisting and snapping in the breeze. "It's not so bad," he said across the miles to Will. "You wouldn't have been so scared." But he wondered if that was true.

"Wait, what happened to the village?" one of the riders asked. Bert followed his pointing finger. He saw no village—only heaps of blackened timbers and charred, sagging walls. Dozens of them.

"Didn't ya hear?" another rider answered. "Lord Charmaigne burned it a month ago."

"What'd he do that for?" said the first.

"Well, you know Hugh Charmaigne. He—" The rider lopped off his words when he realized Bert was listening. *Later*, he mouthed to the other.

Bert's brow furrowed as he stared at the blackened

bones of the little town. Just a few weeks ago it must have been like the quiet clusters of huts and cottages that surrounded Ambercrest, home to shepherds and farmers. *Fishermen, too*, he thought, looking at the shallow, reedy lake on the far side of the ruined village. He wondered what became of all its people.

A single outer wall surrounded the castle. Lord Charmaigne was at the open gate when the carriage pulled up, with a pack of enormous hunting dogs at his side. Bert recognized his uncle's curdled face from that one visit to The Crags and the handful of times he and Aunt Elaine had come to Ambercrest. Bert was not fond of the man. Who was? Hugh Charmaigne was ill-tempered, but in a different way from the baron. While Bert's father bellowed and blustered, his uncle stewed and griped. Months ago Bert and Will overheard Mother talking about their uncle. She was telling a friend that Hugh Charmaigne was obviously jealous of his younger brother. But honestly, she said, who could blame him? Walter had gotten the best of him in every way. Walter was taller, stronger, more eloquent and handsome. More *noble*. The king certainly knew who was the better man. That's why he gave Ambercrest to Walter. If anyone wanted *her* opinion, she thought that Hugh should be quite thankful to have The Crags to rule over, even if it was a remote and dank place with such an . . . *unsavory* history.

Uncle Hugh had on a sour expression as he listened to the baron's men and asked them questions. After the men were dismissed to lead their horses to the stables, he turned to the carriage.

"Are you going to come out, or do you intend to pass the entire summer in your fancy wagon?"

Bert had been waiting. The driver should have climbed down and opened the door for him. That was the proper thing to do. With a sigh he pushed it open and stepped out to stand before his uncle. He looked up at the driver's perch. He intended to flash Matthias a peeved expression until he saw the fellow tugging at his collar and staring anxiously at the savage-looking dogs.

He heard his uncle clear his throat impatiently, so he bowed. It wasn't a deep bow or a long one. It was the least he could get away with without being openly rude, but he didn't care. His mood was as dark as a starless night. When he straightened up again, the look on his uncle's face—a sneer on the lips, one eye almost shut—told him it hadn't gone unnoticed. One of the dogs growled as if it too understood the slight.

"Hello, Uncle," Bert said.

Uncle Hugh sniffed. "Well, Nephew. At least you're not bawling your eyes out this time." He chuckled at his own joke, flashing an irregular row of blackened teeth, and then his native unpleasant expression returned. "Let us get some things understood from the start. I've gotten wind of your reputation. The smell carries all the way from Ambercrest when the breeze is right. And while my brother may spare the rod when it comes to those sorts of antics, I will not. Do you understand me, Will?"

Bert winced. This would not be a good start. He and Will had decided to keep the secret only until Bert made it to The Crags. They figured that once Bert arrived, their parents wouldn't switch them back—they'd be too embarrassed to admit that they'd been duped. *Might as well get this over with*, he thought. "I understand, Uncle," he said. "I'm not Will, though. I'm Bert."

"Bert?" Uncle Hugh needed a moment to recover from this revelation. His lower jaw thrust forward. "We were told that Will would be the one."

"Will was afraid, so I came instead."

"Oh." His uncle narrowed both eyes. "With your father's permission?"

Bert swallowed hard. "Father knows," he said. *He does by now, anyway*, he thought.

Uncle Hugh's head tilted to one side. "And why was your brother afraid to come?"

"Well, because of what they say about this place . . ." Bert began. Then he realized he might be treading on dangerous ground. He fumbled for words. "Um, I mean, without me, he was worried about leaving Ambercrest— that's just how he is. . . ."

"Listen, boy," his uncle snapped, eager to take offense, "the only thing that frightens us here is what just rolled up on four wheels. But you won't give us any trouble, I promise you that. In fact, we might as well make the rules clear right now. Are you listening?"

"Yes, Uncle," said Bert, but he didn't hear much after that. As Uncle Hugh droned on—no wandering the castle after dark, do what you're told, dress properly at all times—Bert glanced over his uncle's shoulder, up at The Crags. It was like something he might have dreamed about. That terrace—is that where the Witch-Queen stood to keep a jealous eye on her beautiful stepdaughter walking in the courtyard below? *Emelina . . . Snow White . . .*

Uncle Hugh's voice intruded again. "And above all, you will speak respectfully to me and your aunt. That is, when we ask you to speak. Otherwise you shouldn't speak at all. Is all this clear or do I need to write it down for you?"

"I understand the rules, Uncle." He'd have figured them out soon enough. Breaking them was always a good way to finding out what they were.

"Good. Your aunt will show you to your quarters. You—I suppose you need to eat. Come with me," Uncle Hugh said to Matthias. Hugh Charmaigne strutted away, and the huge dogs loped behind him.

Bert counted them as they walked away. *Five . . . six . . . seven . . . eight.* When Bert was here years ago, those dogs seemed like monsters to him. They didn't look so different now. The tips of their ears—ears as big as his hands—reached as high as his uncle's chest. Father had told him once that Hugh Charmaigne was determined to own the largest, fiercest hunting dogs in the land. He'd seize any large specimens that his subjects owned and breed them at The Crags. When the pups were twelve weeks old, he'd pluck out the one or two largest, then ordered the rest to be drowned. It was rumored that he'd even mixed wolf blood into the line.

Whatever Hugh Charmaigne was doing, it was working. *I could ride one of those things if you put a saddle on it*, Bert thought.

Aunt Elaine waited for him at the door to the keep. Unlike his mother, who adorned herself with all the jewels she could bear, Aunt Elaine could have been taken for a commoner. Her hair hung limp and straight, not swept up and pinned into an artful construction. Her lips and cheeks and eyelids were unpainted, and the sun had bronzed her skin. She didn't reek of perfume. And her dress wasn't the latest thing that merchants had carted up from the fashionable heart of the kingdom. His aunt was not a homely woman; she was lovely in her own way, but it was a forlorn kind of beauty, like a gloomy mist hanging over a lake after a cold autumn night.

Aunt Elaine greeted Bert with a listless smile, and of course she called him Will, so he had to explain the switch all over again. She eyed him quizzically, and then led the way inside.

The interior was as strange as Bert remembered. It was like walking into a hollow mountain. Opposite the entrance there was a wall of solid rock—not the carefully fitted stones of a castle wall, but the natural surface of the ledge itself. A narrow staircase had been hewn by hand along the face of this rock, and Bert followed his aunt to the second level, wondering at the brute force that it must have taken to carve out those steps.

"This is where you will stay," she said, opening a door. Bert wasn't sure what to expect, but it wasn't this. The room was huge, even larger than the chamber where Mother and Father slept. Tapestries covered every wall, aged and tattered, but still glorious with the deepest greens, crimsons, purples, and golds. The largest one featured a striking red rose in full bloom, surrounded by buds and tiny leaves and branches with wicked thorns.

The room had received some attention in recent hours. Some of the thick wooden planks on the floor were still damp from a scrubbing, and crushed herbs had been sprinkled upon them. The blankets on the bed looked clean. Still, a million particles of dust were suspended in the shafts of sunlight that stabbed through the single wide window at the end of the room. And the scent of herbs could not mask the stench of mouse and must. It was clear that no one had stayed in this place for years.

"Whose room was this?" asked Bert, giving his itchy nose a vigorous rub.

"At first your uncle and I slept here," his aunt said. "It was the master chamber, after all. But after the children, I could not be happy here anymore. Did you know about the children?" She stared at Bert. He widened his eyes and shook his head.

"Well, you were young yourself, I suppose," she said. "Still, I thought your mother might have mentioned it." Aunt Elaine sighed and blinked once, slowly. "We had three babies. All were born in this room. And all . . . all three passed away in this room, before their first month. I thought perhaps we could change our luck if we changed our rooms. And in a way we did. After that, no more babies were born at all." Bert had no idea what to say or do. He cleared his throat and rubbed one arm with the opposite hand. His aunt stared at a corner of the room and tapped her belly lightly with the fingers of one hand. The moment seemed eternal, but then she startled Bert when she spoke again with forced cheer. "I forgot— I have something you might like. I'll be right back."

Aunt Elaine came back holding a tall, bell-shaped wooden cage with a finch inside. It was a pretty creature with yellow and black wings. As she walked, it clung to its perch and flapped its wings to hold its balance. "To brighten your room," she said. "I hope you like it."

"I do," said Bert. Without really thinking about it, he hugged his aunt. She gave him a smile that, this time, was not listless at all.

His aunt left after telling him that dinner would be ready before long. When the door closed, Bert picked up the cage and peered at the bird. "Hello in there. Would you sing for me? No? Would you like to see our room, then?" He walked around the perimeter of the chamber with the birdcage, holding it high and coaxing the creature with whistles. The bird suddenly leaped off its perch and chirped madly, hammering its wings against the bars of the cage.

"It's all right!" Bert said. He tried to shush the bird, but it grew even wilder. Tiny feathers and bits of down fluttered from the cage. Bert thought Aunt Elaine might know what to do, so he ran to the door. But before he reached it the bird calmed itself and returned to its swinging perch. "What an ill-tempered little beast," he said. "Perhaps I should name you Hugh." He half expected to hear Will's laugh ring out beside him, and felt the stab of his brother's absence once more.

Bert carried the cage to a low table at the side of his bed, and the bird seemed content. It groomed its ruffled feathers with its beak, and in time the rapid thumping of its breast subsided.

Bert ate his dinner quietly, trying not to draw his uncle's attention. Uncle Hugh crunched and smacked and slurped his meal while the dogs loitered under the table and around his chair, fighting over the crumbs he spilled and the bones he tossed over his shoulder. He occasionally glanced at Bert with narrowed eyes, hoping perhaps to catch him doing something—anything—wrong.

Uncle Hugh seemed only to enjoy himself once, when a mewing kitten wandered into the hall and the snarling hounds chased after it. Bert wanted badly to rescue the kitten, but he knew better than to leave his seat without permission. And when he looked over, his uncle was watching him from the corner of his eye.

After dinner Bert wandered into the courtyard. The last words his father said were like an echo that never faded away. So the barony might not be his to inherit?

Bert felt an ache in his jaw and realized he'd been clenching his teeth. *I'll just have to prove myself*, he thought, rubbing his cheeks with his fingertips. *I'll stay out of trouble. Father will see I'm not as rash as he thinks. But that's not all. If Uncle Hugh is up to something, I'll find out what it is.*

The days were long, and there was still plenty of sunlight after the dinner hour. He went out to the courtyard and was struck again by a difference between this place and his home. Ambercrest was more than just a soaring castle between broad walls. It was the heart of a bustling community, surrounded by villages and pastures, and populated by farmers, merchants, craftsmen, millers, butchers, smiths, bakers, and countless others. The Crags wasn't like that. This was more like a garrison, a grim stronghold on the fringe of the kingdom, the last stop before you blundered right off the map into a hostile unknown. And there was nobody here but the ill-tempered lord and his glum lady, a handful of dour servants, and armed men.

But how many men? Too many? Enough to cause trouble if a renegade commanded them?

The courtyard of Ambercrest was wide and sunny,

but at The Crags it was merely a dank, narrow alley between the keep and the single wall. Bert circled around the stone structure and found a pointed corner where the courtyard ended abruptly at a wall of natural rock—the mountain itself. Then he turned and walked back, intending to count all the soldiers he saw on the ground and up on the walls. Father said there shouldn't be more than eighty. Bert strolled around, pretending to be bored. It seemed like every man who saw him scowled or turned away. He'd gotten up to fifty when he saw his uncle talking with another group of armed men. *That makes fifty-five already*, he thought. *Not counting who's in the barracks or on patrol . . .*

The dogs were there too, as usual. As soon as Uncle Hugh saw Bert, he turned his back and lowered his voice, and the soldiers tightened their circle. Bert stretched his arms and yawned loudly, but his heart thumped against his ribs. Perhaps his uncle was up to no good after all.

Uncle Hugh walked farther around the curve of the keep, followed by his dogs and the circle of men. Bert clasped his hands behind his back, whistled quietly, and ambled in that direction. When he was near the corner, a voice came from above. "I wouldn't if I were you."

Bert turned his crimson face toward the voice. Aunt Elaine was there, hanging a basket of cascading yellow flowers from the balcony. "Wouldn't do what?" he asked, with more edge to his voice than he intended. He added an awkward, belated smile.

"Follow your uncle," she said. "He wouldn't like it. Trust me."

"I wasn't following him! I'm just trying to learn my way around," Bert said.

"Why don't you learn your way upstairs and give me a hand?" she replied.

Bert was with her a few minutes later on the wide terrace atop the keep. The place was littered with benches and tables and shelves. Plants were everywhere. Seedlings sprouted in trays; bushes grew in halved barrels; flowers hung from baskets; strange, fat, prickly plants sat in buckets of sand; and vines crawled up trellises and rock walls.

"Hello, Aunt Elaine," he said. "What's all this for?"

His aunt plucked an oval leaf from the plant she was potting. She crushed it between her fingers and brought it to her nose to inhale deeply. "Some will bring flavor to our dishes. Some are said to have healing properties. And others will brighten this gloomy place with their blossoms."

Gloomy is right, Bert thought, looking at the rocky peaks that cast shadows on The Crags for too many hours each day. His gaze followed the slope all the way down to where it reached the edge of the ruined village. "Why did Uncle Hugh burn it?" he said.

His aunt frowned. "He got . . . ," she started, but her voice faltered. She pressed her lips together, cleared her throat, and began again. "He got the idea that those people were conspiring with the Dwergh."

Bert nearly hopped with excitement. "Really? Why did he think that?"

"One of his soldiers insisted he'd seen someone talking in the valley to a Dwergh. Of course, the soldier saw it from far away. And he couldn't find the Dwergh or the person when he chased them. But that was enough evidence for my husband." Aunt Elaine crossed her arms and stared at the village. "Something about The Crags scares people, Bert. And that brings out the worst in them."

Bert straightened his back and raised his chin. "It doesn't scare me. I'm not afraid of the Dwergh. And I don't believe all those stories about the Witch-Queen."

His aunt wiped her hands on her apron. "You shouldn't believe all of them. It happened too long ago. But some of the stories—even the worst of them—are true. And it's a sadder tale than you've imagined, Nephew. A far sadder tale."

CHAPTER
6

*H*ow? *How could I let Bert take my place?* Will lay on his bed with his pillow clamped over his eyes. He wondered if he would sleep better tonight, or if it would be like last night, when he kept waking, hoping that everything that happened over the last two days was merely a nightmare. He'd called Bert's name, and when there was no answer, he crept over in the dark and ran his hands across the empty bed.

I can't bear this, he thought. He and Bert had scarcely spent an hour apart since they were born. And now, a whole summer? An infinity of days stretched before him, and every minute so far had been torture.

"I am so sorry," he said drowsily. He shouldn't have let Bert sneak down to look at the maps or climb out the window to spy on their parents. And he never should have let him go in his place to The Crags. If he was ever going to tell his brother no, that had been the moment. The Crags! There was danger there. Will knew there was; he could feel the menace from across the miles. And if trouble was there, of course Bert would find it. He was adventurous. He was curious. He was clever. *Don't*

49

explore, Will called out wordlessly. *Don't poke around.*

Images played across Will's mind as he drifted along the foggy shore between wakefulness and sleep. He saw walls part, revealing a secret place as dark as night. He saw Bert walk into the dark place, and Will tried to call a warning, but he couldn't make sounds come out of his mouth. In this dream he'd forgotten how to speak. Something frightened Bert, something beyond the blackness that Will could not see, and Bert whirled around to get away. There was a hiss and a squeal of fear, the kind an animal might make in the jaws of a wolf. Whatever was behind Bert dragged him backward. Bert reached toward Will, pleading with his eyes as the darkness devoured him. . . .

Will ripped the pillow from his eyes and lurched upright. Now that he was awake he found his voice again. He used it to scream.

CHAPTER
7

Bert wasn't sure why he was awake. One moment he was sound asleep and the next his eyes snapped open, just like that.

He became aware of a noise in the darkness, so faint that he could not even rustle his blanket if he wanted to hear it. It came from outside his room: the mew of a kitten. In the narrow space under his door, he saw the shadows of four tiny legs.

He kicked off the blankets and crossed the room with the dry herbs crunching under his bare feet and catching between his toes. He opened the door carefully—the hinges creaked dreadfully—and looked out. At his feet he saw the kitten that the hounds had chased. It took a few wobbly steps in the other direction. Bert kneeled down and scooped it up. He slipped the kitten into a fold of his nightshirt and cradled it with one arm. Then he took the extinguished candle from his room and crept down the hall to use one of the lamps there to light the wick. He was relieved to make it safely back and close the groaning door behind him. No doubt stepping out of his room after dark would be a serious breach of one of Uncle Hugh's "rules."

Settling back into bed, he let the kitten out of its cocoon. It was a she-cat, black with white legs and a white chin. He whispered to her and scratched behind her ears. The kitten soon relaxed, and she tilted her head to offer her cheek and neck to Bert's fingers. Before long her eyes closed, and she curled up in the nook between Bert's pillow and his shoulder, purring furiously. Bert fell asleep thinking about how much his brother loved animals.

Not long after that he woke for the second time that night. The kitten bounded across the bed, chasing a moth that fluttered around the candle. Bert grinned as he watched her little head swivel around to track the flight of the moth, and he laughed out loud when the moth flew directly over the kitten and caused her to topple over backward as she pawed wildly at the air. The moth headed for safer territory at the other end of the room. The kitten leaped off the bed to follow.

Near the far wall, the kitten stopped in front of the tapestry of the rose. Bert laughed again—her tiny tail had puffed out, doubling in size. She arched her back, and the fur along her spine bristled. Then she turned sideways, a ludicrous attempt to make herself look bigger.

"What's the matter with you?" Bert said, climbing out of bed. "Are all the animals here crazy?" He gently picked her up again, and she scrambled to free herself from his grip. Her tiny claws were sharp as needles, as sharp as those thorns looked in the tapestry of roses in front of Bert.

Roses. A thought occurred to Bert. Didn't the bird panic at the same place, in front of that tapestry with the great blooming flower? The kitten still clawed madly, so Bert held her away from his body and brought her back to the bed. But she wouldn't stay. She jumped down and ran to the door, trying to push her nose into the space below, frantic to leave.

Bert watched the kitten, but then his eyes went back to the tapestry. He picked up the birdcage from the table by his bed. Holding the cage in front of him with a hand on each side, he walked toward the woven image of the rose. When he was four steps away, the bird began to fidget on its perch. When he was two steps away, the bird screeched and flew, once, twice, three times into the narrow bars, its wings a blur. He backed away and put the cage back on the table, and the bird settled down.

Bert drew in a great breath and let it out in a whoosh. *What's happening here?*

He brought the candle close to scan the tapestry, but saw nothing unusual. He sniffed it warily, wondering if the animals had picked up some offensive odor— something one of Uncle Hugh's dogs had done, maybe. But there was nothing that he could detect except the smell of great age—the tapestry might have hung there for a hundred years. He ran his free hand across it, feeling the intricate weave under his fingertips. He pressed his palm against it and felt unrelenting stone behind the fabric.

Bert pursed his lips and lowered his brow. He pulled the tapestry away from the wall on one side and peered behind it. There was an ominous creak and a whoosh from above, and he covered his head with his arms as the entire tapestry crashed down. The fabric made little noise, but the wooden bar that it was suspended from hit the floor with an astounding clatter.

Bert let out a curse he'd heard his father use more than once. He raced to his bed and climbed under the covers, ready to snuff out the candle. If anyone came to investigate the noise, he'd pretend to be disoriented and sleepy as if the tapestry had fallen on its own.

No one came. He thought he heard running footsteps in some distant part of The Crags, but there was no knock on his door. He waited to be certain. Then he returned to kneel beside the crumpled tapestry. It didn't seem to be damaged. Looking up he saw that it had slipped off a hook on the wall—he could mount it again if he stood on a chair.

The wall was easier to inspect with the tapestry down, though. Nothing he could see explained the behavior of the bird and the kitten. The wall was made of great square blocks of stone, expertly fitted. The surface was so smooth that he was compelled to touch it. He drew his flattened palm across the cold stone, and a curious thing happened: a gentle, invisible tug at his hand.

"Huh?" He moved his palm back across the stone and felt it again—something pulling, not at his finger, but at the iron ring he wore. "Lodestone," he whispered, remembering something a peddler had once sold him and Will. It was a magical kind of ore that pulled on anything made of iron, and attracted or repelled other bits of the same stuff.

He put his nose an inch from the wall, peered carefully, and saw an edge as thin as a hair around the spot he had just touched. The area was shaped like a teardrop, and as big as his fingertip. When he pressed it, the spot sunk into the wall as if there was a spring behind it. It was so strange and unexpected that he laughed out loud.

He took off his ring and slid it across the stone in every direction. Soon he found two more teardrop shapes just like the first. Together with the first spot they formed a triangle, large enough for his open hand to fit inside its center.

"Weird," he said. He wondered if his aunt and uncle knew about it. Probably not, he decided. He'd found it purely by accident—he could have easily missed it. And the tapestry that covered the triangle looked like it had been there forever, concealing this strange secret. "But what's it for?"

Now there *were* footsteps approaching. Bert pulled a chair over to the wall, lifted the tapestry, and set it back on its hook. The steps were getting closer and louder, and he heard muttering voices. He flew across the room and into bed. He licked his fingertips with his tongue and pinched out the flame of the candle, so it wouldn't send up a stream of telltale smoke. Then he flopped back and squeezed his eyes closed as his door began to open.

CHAPTER
8

Will dipped his pen into the jar of ink and began to write.

> Dear Brother,
>   I hope everything is well with you. Parley says he will hurry to bring you this letter without wasting time along the way like he usually does. He is a good friend. Right after you left I ran into him. I was still pretending to be you, but he gave me a squinty look and a strange smile as if he knew that something was up. His one eye is better than our parents' four!
>   I suppose you're wondering how things went when I told Father and Mother that we switched places. I waited two days, like we agreed. Then I told them during dinner. Mother moaned and dropped her head into her hands. Father started cursing. I thought he might tear his beard out. Then he did something strange. He got very quiet and said to himself, "That was Bert in the carriage, not you? But I told him . . ." And then he knocked his

57

goblet off the table. What on Earth did he say
to you? I'm sure it was something awful about me.
Don't let it bother you. Anyway, he told me to go
to our room. An hour later he kicked the door
open, stormed in, and started shouting again.
So you thought you'd take Bert's place, eh? Fine,
you'll do just that. I brought a tutor all the way
to Ambercrest to teach Bert to fight. And you'll
be his student, like it or not!"

So we were right about one thing: They won't
make us change places again. Just like we guessed,
they don't want to admit to Uncle Hugh that we
fooled them.

Now I have to take the fighting lessons that were
meant for you, from some knight named Andreas.
You're probably sorry to miss that, and I bet
you're laughing at me. I don't want the lessons,
but I have no choice.

Will's pen paused over the parchment. He gnawed his
bottom lip and went on writing.

Bert, I had a terrible dream last night, that
something bad happened to you. It made me feel
awful that I let you go instead of me. The Crags is
a strange place. I hope you will be careful there. Do
me a favor—don't poke around in dark corners.
I'm going to stay out of trouble here. I'll even

take the stupid lessons without complaining. And
you should behave yourself too. If we're good, maybe
Father and Mother will let you come home in a few
weeks instead of staying the whole summer.
 I miss you. Be careful.
 Your brother,
 Will

CHAPTER
9

Bert followed his aunt down the dark corridor. She wouldn't tell him where she was bringing him; she only promised he'd find it interesting.

If it wasn't for her, nobody would talk to him. Uncle Hugh treated him like a nuisance, and the rest of the people in the castle—soldiers and servants alike—were careful to avoid him, fearful of Lord Charmaigne's wrath. But not Aunt Elaine.

"You and Uncle Hugh . . . ," Bert started to say without really thinking. He coughed and completed his thought. "You're not much alike."

She looked amused as she stopped to look back at him. "That's true enough. I realized the same thing the moment I met him, on our wedding day."

Bert's jaw went slack. "You didn't meet him till you married him?"

She shook her head. "The marriage wasn't my decision, of course. It was my father's and your grandfather's. But now I belong to Hugh," she said. She turned and continued down the corridor, adding quietly, as if to herself, "And he doesn't part with what he owns."

The corridor soon ended at a small wooden door. Aunt Elaine produced a key from a pocket at her waist, slipped it into the keyhole and turned it. It opened into a windowless room in the back of the keep.

"What's in there?" he asked.

"You seem curious about the history of The Crags and the Witch-Queen. I thought this would interest you." Aunt Elaine went in first, holding one hand in front of her face. Bert wondered why until he felt a fine strand of spider silk on his cheek. He lifted his hand the same way.

The room was full of old things coated with dust. Furniture. Works of art. Moldy pennants. Rusted armor. Unknown objects covered by cloth. Padlocked chests filled with who-knows-what.

Aunt Elaine crisscrossed the room using her candle's flame to light others that were spread about the place. The candles in the nearest corner were held by the most unusual candlestick Bert had ever seen. It was a three-legged sculpture that looked as if a trio of iron snakes balanced on their tails and curled around one another in the center. A candle was thrust into each open jaw. As they slowly burned, it would look as if the serpents were devouring them.

There were dozens of curious objects in the room, but he found himself drawn to the candlestick. He wasn't sure why. It seemed important. Significant. He traced his fingertip along one of the sculpted snakes, starting at the gaping mouth. When his finger reached the other end, he felt a tug on his ring, and it stuck with a *clack* against the tip of the tail.

"What's the matter, Bert?" Aunt Elaine said.

"What?" he replied in a voice that squeaked.

"Just now it looked like your eyes might pop out of your face. Did something scare you?"

"No," he said, forcing a laugh. He lifted the candlestick and gave it a look that was meant to convey indifference. "My room gets pretty dark, Aunt Elaine. Do you think I could use this while I'm here?"

"If you'd like," she said. "It belonged to her, you know. Like everything else in here." She swept her arm toward the center of the room where an elaborate chair stood. Bert went to take a closer look. The chair was carved out of deep-brown wood, with broad, curving arms and a tall back that he could just reach the top of when he went up on his toes and stretched his arm. Near the throne's head he slipped his fingers into empty notches the size of walnuts. Whatever was in there once had been pried out. He saw pale scars around the gaps, where someone's blade had dug and scratched.

"That was her throne. It was once encrusted with jewels. Until my husband plucked them out," Aunt Elaine said. Her lip curled up on one side for a moment. Then she took a deep breath. "I'm sure you've heard that the Witch-Queen was beautiful," she said. "Would you like to see her?"

"I guess," Bert said. Aunt Elaine went to a corner of the room where a series of gilded frames stood like a row of books. She drew out one of the tallest ones and carried it to the throne, keeping the painted side of the canvas turned away from Bert. Then she propped the picture across the arms of the throne and said, "Rohesia."

It's true, Bert thought. *She was beautiful.* He was suddenly aware that his head had listed to one side as he beheld her painted image. He blinked hard and stood straight.

The artist was skilled, that was certain; far better than the amateur who had infuriated his mother a few years back and was banished from the barony under the threat of torture. The Witch-Queen sat on a simple, armless chair. She held a cluster of leafy branches in her hands, and across her lap were the dried stems, leaves, berries, and roots of a variety of plants. At her side was a bench cluttered with potted plants and watering cans. Behind her was a garden in full bloom. Bert peered at the lovely face, eye-high with his own. The complexion was fair, the features fine. Her auburn hair was tied back with a ribbon and adorned with a simple coronet. Her thin, red lips were turned up in a smile, a warm and cheery smile that crinkled the corners of her eyes.

"Not exactly the portrait of evil," Aunt Elaine said.

"No," Bert replied. In fact, this looked like someone you'd want to have for a friend, as long as you weren't daunted by her beauty. "But artists do that," Bert said.

"They lie with paint. They make you look better than you do in real life. They leave out the warts and the scars. They can leave out evil, just the same."

"Is that so?" Aunt Elaine said. "Then why did he paint her like this?" She pointed toward the Witch-Queen's hands. Bert leaned in close, and his eyebrows rose. The hands were dirty. The nails were unpainted, and dirt was caked underneath. "Why . . . ?" he said.

Aunt Elaine went back to the paintings and withdrew the largest frame from the stack. "The same man painted this, just two years later."

Bert's brow furrowed. It was the same woman. But transformed somehow. She was on her throne now—the very seat where her portrait was now propped. But the empty notches on the chair were filled with glittering gems. Her posture was rigid and formal. There were no dirty hands this time—long, perfect, ruby-red nails gripped the arms of the throne like the talons of a bird of prey. All the warmth was gone from her features. There was a smile on her red lips, but devoid of happiness. The cold stare in her eye made Bert shiver. No, this painter left nothing out. The Witch-Queen was evil, the artist perceived it, and his brush told the truth.

"What . . . happened to her?"

"Nobody knows. Rohesia was a healer, Bert, not a murderess—at least not until the last years of her life. True, she'd always taken pride in her beauty. Look at her—who wouldn't be proud of that face, that form?

But until the end there was something more important in her life. She spent her days learning how to treat the ill and the infirm with herbs and compounds. The gardens of The Crags were filled with the plants she grew for their medicinal qualities. And her shelves were filled with extracts from bark and berry and root and leaf, each with their own power to cure. She drew her knowledge from ancient books and from the poor but wise folk who lived in these lands. She was even a friend to the Dwergh. She reached out to them because she knew there were healers among them, and she wanted to share knowledge that might benefit both of our peoples. In return for the secrets to their medicines, she allowed Dwergh parties to come and mine our lands.

"That is the Rohesia that everyone has forgotten: the kind ruler, the person who only wanted to heal. It was only in her final years that she became the hateful Witch-Queen, jealous of anyone whose beauty approached her own. But now the murderess is all that anyone can recall. I had to search long and hard, and talk to the very oldest people in these parts, to learn about the good queen. You see, Bert, in the end, the evil you've done is always remembered more vividly than the good."

Bert lifted the first painting out and set it in front of the other. He looked again at the long sprigs of unknown plants that Rohesia held in her lap. *Rohesia the healer.* No, nobody ever talked about that at Ambercrest.

"I've wondered for years what drove her mad," Aunt

Elaine said. "I believe her mind might have been poisoned by one of the exotic plants that she cultivated. What else could explain it?"

"Maybe you're right," Bert said, looking into the tenderly painted eyes. It was as good a guess as any.

"Still . . . the rumors about her are so strange. Everything I learned was passed down through generations, so I'm not certain how much to believe. Especially the tales of her dark magic. They say that Rohesia could bewitch men, crush their will and turn them into mindless slaves who would do her bidding no matter how grim or wicked the task. They say that she kept horrible beasts for pets, misshapened things that were only glimpsed from afar, because anyone who saw them close up perished under their teeth and claws. They say she would lock herself in her room for days—the very room where you're staying now, Bert. The servants would wonder if she needed help, and they would knock on the door, but there would be no answer and not a sound from within—as if she had vanished like a ghost. Whether those things are true, I do not know. But it can't be denied that many folk who defied her met grisly fates. Or that she went mad with jealousy and tried to kill her own stepdaughter, Snow White."

In the silence that followed, Bert looked again at the friendly, lovely face in the first painting. He took a deep, long breath. "Still," he said, "at least she gathered all that knowledge . . ."

"That's the saddest part," Aunt Elaine said. She brushed a strand of hair away from her eyes. Bert noticed dirt under her fingernails. "Most of the wisdom she collected was somehow lost. Only a few of her notes remain. I would give anything to find the rest, Bert. Anything."

CHAPTER
10

Bert was almost out of parchment, and his hand was cramped, but there was so much more to tell his brother. He clenched and unclenched his fingers to ease the soreness, and then went on writing.

> As soon as I got back to my room, I closed the door and went behind the rose tapestry. You can probably guess what happened next. The candlestick was like a key! When I turned it the right way, all three snake tails stuck to the three spots on the wall, just like those old bits of lodestone we used to play with. I pushed, and all three tails sank into the wall. Then I heard sounds, like chains moving behind the wall, and part of the wall swung inward, just like a door. It was amazing! The stones opened farther and farther, and when they finally stopped, there was an opening big enough to get through.
>
> I know you think nothing scares me, but I have to admit that I was afraid to go through that doorway. Do you know what I finally did? I pretended

you were right behind me, just like always. I lit a candle and went through. I was worried someone might come in and learn the secret. But even if they did, they probably wouldn't find it. The tapestry covered the whole thing, and as far as anyone knows, it's a solid wall back there!

It was dark and cold inside, and there was a strange smell. My hand shook so hard I was afraid I would drop my candle.

Do you know that I wasn't even in the castle anymore? Once I passed through that wall, I was in the cliffs behind The Crags. Everything around me was carved right out of rock! It was so dark. It was as if the blackness was hungry, and it ate the light from my candle. There was a short landing at the top of the opening, and then stairs. They went down a long way—I could not see the bottom from where I was.

You should have seen what I saw. Even though it was blacker than coal, there were little bits of flat, glassy stuff in the rock, and they caught the light of my candle. It looked as if thousands of stars twin-kled all around me. I call it the "Tunnel of Stars." I went down the steps, and they kept going and going. There was a room at the bottom. Or it might have been a cave. It was hard to tell what was natural and what was carved from the stone. Just imagine—long ago someone tunneled all the way to

*that cave. I wonder if you even believe me as you
read this, but it is true. I wish you could come, so I
could show you.*

*Someone used this place as a hideaway. You
know who that must have been! To think that I
sleep in her room, and now I've found her hidden
chamber. I did not see any witchy stuff down there.
Perhaps Father is right, and she was not a witch at
all. There was hardly anything in the cave. Just a
chair and some lamps she must have used to light
the place.*

Bert stopped writing. There was something else down
there, of course. But for some reason he hesitated to
include it in the letter. Why? He shook his head and
chided himself. What secrets could he keep from his
twin? They knew everything about each other. They
always had. Of course he'd write about it.

*There was also a mirror at the very end of the
chamber. It is filthy, but I may try to clean it. There
is a table next to the mirror, with some combs that
look like they are made of bone. I almost expected to
see the Witch-Queen's ghost sitting there, looking at
herself in that mirror and brushing her hair!*

*I am almost out of parchment now, and it is late,
so I think I will end this letter. Uncle Hugh said I
should give him any notes I want to send, and he*

will give them to the courier. But I do not trust
him. I think he would read the letter himself first!
I do miss you, and I think about you always.
Sometimes I get the feeling that you are thinking
about me. I wonder if you get the same feeling.
Good-bye for now, Brother, and be brave.
Remember that everything I have written is
a secret. Hide this letter, or better yet burn it,
and tell no one.

Bert signed the letter and set the last page beside the others to dry, considering what he had written about the mirror. And what he had not written.

He had not written that a magnificent chair was arranged in front of the mirror, so that a person could sit and gaze directly at his reflection. And he had not written that this chair, with its wide seat and soaring back and brawny arms, was more majestic than Father's throne or Uncle Hugh's unimpressive seat.

He hadn't written that the mirror was breathtaking and certainly priceless. Its frame looked as if it was made of solid gold, inlaid with silver so pure and white that it seemed to glow. He hadn't written that the silver was in the shape of symbols—some form of writing that was exotic and unfamiliar.

Nor had he written that when he used his sleeve to rub at the dusty glass, the reflection in that clean patch was amazing in its clarity. It was nothing like the polished sheets of silver or brass that served for mirrors at Ambercrest, sadly distorting the face of anyone who looked into them. He wasn't certain, but it may have been the kind of mirror that Mother always talked about. Those mirrors came from someplace far away, and they were made with a special kind of glass and a secret process, jealously guarded. They were so rare and priceless that the only person in the kingdom who had one was the king himself.

When the ink was dry, Bert gathered the pages together. He stood and hesitated. Suddenly he had an urge—almost overwhelming—to tear the letter into pieces and let the candle consume the scraps one by one.

But why would I do anything like that? he wondered, shaking his head and blinking hard. Of course he'd share this secret with his brother. Not everything, perhaps. After all these years of being side by side for every experience, there was something wonderful about having part of it, even a small part, to himself. Will could learn the rest in time.

Bert rolled the pages and tied a ribbon around them. He dribbled wax from the candle across the ribbon. Then he pressed his iron ring onto the wax, leaving an impression of the family crest. There was nothing sacred or official about this seal, but perhaps Uncle Hugh would think twice before breaking it to read the letter, if he managed to intercept it.

Hugh Charmaigne. How satisfying it was to have

discovered this secret, right under his pig nose. Uncle Hugh had watched Bert's every move with cold suspicion, looking for an excuse to banish him to his room. Bert laughed at the thought. *Go ahead and punish me! There's no place I'd rather be.*

For now, he had to figure out how to get the letter directly to the courier. If his father sent Parley, that would solve the problem. Parley could be trusted. He hid the letter under his bed and left the room. He was anxious to see if a courier had arrived.

He was eager, too, for night to come and the others to sleep. Because when they did, he would unlock the hidden door again, go down through the Tunnel of Stars, and wash the mirror.

11

"Parley!"

Tom Parley looked drained from the long ride under a roasting sun, but his sweaty, round face broke into a wide grin when he saw Bert running his way.

Parley was one of the baron's men, but a soldier no more. His brief career as a fighter hadn't gone well. In short order he lost an eye; broke an arm that never healed properly and shriveled a bit; and snapped a leg that didn't mend well either, so that he forever after walked with a pronounced limp. But Parley was earnest and reliable and cheerful. The baron valued the earnestness and reliability, and he tolerated the cheerfulness. Parley was now employed as one of the messengers who crisscrossed the land between Ambercrest and the rest of the barony.

"Will, my favorite twin! I like you so much better than your rotten brother." Parley looked at him with his head turned slightly to one side, using his right eye to see. The lid of the missing left eye was permanently closed, so that he seemed to always wink at the world.

"You know who I am, and you're not one bit funny!" Bert smacked him on the chest with an open palm. Parley had joked this way for as long as he could remember. But in truth, this jest stung more than a little. It made Bert remember his last conversation with his father.

"I hope you're proud of yourself, Bert," Parley said. "I heard your father's head nearly burst into flame when he learned about the switch." The courier chuckled and gazed at the ancient castle. "So—enjoying yourself at The Crags?"

"Well, it's actually sort of exciting and mysterious. But I miss Will."

"And he misses you, my boy. But I'll let him tell you." Parley had a leather bag across his shoulder. He drew a letter from it and handed it to Bert.

"Thank you, Parley!" Bert dropped his voice to a whisper. "And I need you to bring one to Will. But I can't give it to you when Uncle is around."

"Then I'll take it just before I leave tomorrow, because here he comes. He's the tallest one in the group, right?" Bert looked behind him and grinned. Hugh Charmaigne was approaching, and as usual his pack of hulking dogs loped beside him.

"Yes," Bert said in a low voice. "He's also the least intelligent." Lord Charmaigne looked at the letter from Will in Bert's hand and gave him an unpleasant stare before asking Parley for news from Ambercrest.

Almost forgot, Bert thought. He'd been neglecting his mission to find out if his uncle was plotting against Ambercrest. Well, that would have to wait. All Bert could think about right now was his own wonderful secret. *My mirror.*

Will's mouth was desert dry. He grimaced and gulped, and then stepped into the brilliant light of the courtyard. *It's too early to be this hot*, he thought, using a hand to shade his eyes. The sunbaked dirt crunched under his feet. On the far side of the courtyard, near the armory, a man stood with his back to Will, arranging weapons and armor on a wooden table. He was tall, with long legs and a narrow waist that flared into powerful shoulders. He wore a shirt without sleeves, and his leathery arms were covered with the white slashes of old scars. His brown hair hung straight down to his shoulders.

It was a long, slow walk across the courtyard. When Will was a few steps away, the man turned and looked at him with an owl's unflinching stare. He had dark eyes, a crooked, beaten nose, and a thin beard that had started to gray. A sword made of battered wood was in his hands; he planted the dull point in the ground between his feet and leaned on the handle.

Will cleared his throat. "Are you Andreas? The knight?"

The man nodded. "And you must be the baron's son. Though it's a funny thing—you're not the one I was told

I'd be teaching." He inclined his head, looking Will from head to toe and back up again. "It doesn't matter, though, Master William. Anyone can learn to fight. Here, see if you can pick this up."

Andreas had arranged more wooden swords on the table. There were nine of them, side by side, each one a little smaller than the sword before it. He pointed at the largest one.

Will wrapped both hands around the handle and pulled it off the table. He grunted as the point wobbled and sank to the ground. He looked at Andreas and shrugged. "Too heavy."

Andreas squinted at him. "Try the middle one."

Will lifted the sword in the middle of the row. He was able to count to five before it started to droop. A second later its point was in the dirt.

Andreas sighed and picked up the last sword in the line. Will felt his face go warm and his ears tingle. Compared to the long, broad sword that Andreas held in his other hand, this one looked like a whittling knife. "This is as small as they come," Andreas said.

"Fine," Will said through his teeth.

"Now the pads," said Andreas.

"Pads?"

"Put them on. Whichever fit best." The knight pointed his sword at a pile of thick, quilted material: leggings and coats. "A helmet, too."

Will strapped on the heavy garments and stuck one of

the dented, bucket-shaped helmets onto his head. The pads reeked of stale sweat.

"And a buckler," Andreas said, handing him a small, round, wooden shield.

Will slipped his hand through the thick, leather strap on the inside of the buckler. He peered out through the horizontal slot in his helmet and noticed a few of the baron's soldiers milling around the courtyard, looking his way and smirking. *Just wonderful*, he thought. *An audience.* A trickle of sweat ran into the corner of his eye and started to burn.

"Before our lessons truly begin, I want to see what you know," Andreas said. He raised his sword and buckler. "Ready?"

"Wait," said Will. "Aren't you going to wear pads? Or a helmet?"

Andreas allowed himself a tiny smile, the first since they met. "That won't be necessary yet, Master Will. Come on, now. Attack."

Will sighed. He'd made up his mind that he would try his best. He raised the sword over one shoulder and charged. He swung the weapon as he drew close, but Andreas stepped nimbly aside. Will had expected the sword to hit something—the other sword, the buckler, the knight, *anything*—but when it swept through unresisting air, he lost his balance and stumbled to the ground, sending up a cloud of dust. He heard snickers in the distance.

Will couldn't see a thing, and realized that his helmet

had swiveled a quarter turn on his head. He adjusted it
and saw Andreas through the slit, gesturing impatiently
for him to attack again.

Once on his feet he approached slowly. Andreas didn't
move until Will swung his sword again. Then the knight
raised his weapon. When the two pieces of wood clashed,
Will felt a jolt of pain shoot from his hand to his elbow.
He gasped and nearly dropped the sword. Then a deafen-
ing clang rocked his brain. It was as if the helmet was a
bell and his head was its clapper.

"Ow!"

"Use your shield, boy—if this was a real battle, your
head would be rolling in the dust already!" said Andreas,
barely audible over the echoes in Will's brain. "The
buckler, *now!*"

Will threw his shield over his head just in time to
block the next descent of Andreas's heavy wooden
sword. Andreas swung the weapon again, battering the
shield, and all Will could do was try to recover in time
to block the next one. On the third strike he dropped to
one knee. On the fourth he fell to his side. Andreas
stepped back.

"Get up. Try again."

Will struggled to his feet, panting like an overworked
dog. It was oven hot inside the helmet, and sweat gushed
from his armpits. As soon as he steadied himself, Andreas
attacked. The man's sword was everywhere that Will's

buckler was not, smacking his arms, legs, and stomach. It hurt despite the thick padding. The sword came straight down again, and Will just managed to block it. And then Andreas hammered him once more from above as if Will was a tent peg he was driving into the ground. Will's buckler finally cracked in half, and he flopped to the ground. He raised one hand and waved it weakly. Andreas stood over him. His shadow blocked the sun.

"Water," Will croaked. It was the only word he had the energy to say. He heard Andreas walk across the courtyard, crunching the straw, and come back. There was silence, and then a bucketful of water poured through the slit of his helmet. Will sputtered and coughed. He rolled over, pushed onto his knees, and pried the helmet off.

He heard laughter. The baron's soldiers were still nearby. They clutched their stomachs and hit their knees with their fists.

"You there!" Andreas called to them. "Does this amuse you? Perhaps you think you'd fare better!" He took one step in their direction, and his fist tightened on the hilt of his sword.

The men sobered instantly. "No, sir," one of them replied, and he led the others away as if something important had to be done elsewhere.

Andreas looked down at Will again. Will turned his face aside and glared into the distance through the damp hair that hung over his eyes. He felt hot bruises in a dozen places and a piercing pain behind his eyes.

"It was your first lesson. No shame in taking a beating," Andreas said.

Will sniffed loudly.

"Enough rest," Andreas said. "We should continue."

The hot day became a sweltering night at The Crags. It began to rain, but even that did not cool the air.

Late that night, when most slept feverishly with their blankets kicked aside, Bert found cool relief as soon as he stepped into the Tunnel of Stars. He carried a bucket of soapy water in one hand and a lamp in the other. Rags were draped across his shoulder. He counted the steps on the way down. There were forty-nine—enough to bring him past the first floor and into the heart of the ledge that lay below.

There were sounds he didn't notice when he discovered the chamber the night before. Drops of water splashed into puddles on the stone floor. A faint rush of air played like a flute from somewhere overhead. He raised the lamp and saw tiny jagged holes in the ceiling, and strange stone formations that hung like icicles.

Bert put the bucket down in front of the mirror. He marveled at the size of the glass. The bottom of it was at his knees and the top was above his head. He grasped it by the sides and tried to lift it, wondering how heavy it was. *Very,* he thought. He inspected the exquisite frame, to make certain it was not merely carved wood that had been gilded. No, he was sure that all of it was truly gold, even the four sturdy feet, which looked like dragon's claws. The inlaid silver seemed genuine as well. Without question, this was a treasure worth more than anything his parents possessed.

He dunked a rag in the bucket and wiped the face of the mirror. The coat of dirt eagerly slid off. In seconds there was a filthy pool of water at his feet and a tall, sparkling oval of glass before his eyes.

It was the most beautiful thing Bert had ever seen. And his reflection—he'd never beheld himself like this. Keeping his eyes locked on the glass, he stepped back. He reached behind him to find the broad arms of the chair that faced the mirror, and sat down.

He turned his head to examine his profile. He made faces: silly, angry, frightened, serious. He circled his fingers over his eyes like a mask. He stuck his tongue out, and put his thumbs in his ears and waggled his fingers.

Then he sat back and stared. *Is this the face of a baron?* he wondered, and he winced. He wasn't so sure anymore. Just like the barony, that face could easily belong to Will. *We really do look alike. Exactly alike.* His father's words flooded back, and he tried to push them aside.

He thought of Hugh Charmaigne, greedily prying the precious stones out of the Witch-Queen's other throne. *Too bad you never found this chamber, Uncle.* Perhaps there was a way to smuggle the mirror out when he left for home, though he could not imagine how. He'd worry about that later. But he knew one thing: He would never allow Hugh Charmaigne to get his pig hands on this precious thing. *Never!*

Something caught his ear. He sat up and cocked his head to listen better. He still heard the whistle of the wind through the cracks in the cavern's ceiling. But now another sound accompanied it. And this one had a rhythm.

It was a long, low sound of gently rushing air. And then a pause. And then the same sound, but softer this time. It would have been easy to miss. But now that he was aware of the sound, it was all he could hear.

He turned his head to one side, and then the other, listening keenly. He was afraid it would stop before he discovered the source. But it went on repeating like a pair of sighs: low, and lower. Low, and lower.

Inward and outward.

Can it be? The hairs on the back of his neck stood like quills. He stepped out of the chair and put his ear to the cold surface of the mirror. Yes, that was where the sound came from. And he recognized it for what it was.

Breathing.

It wasn't like the rapid, excited breaths that he was taking now. It was more like the relaxed inhalations and exhalations of someone in a deep, deep sleep. The sound was soothing. He kept his ear to the glass for a long time, closed his eyes, and just listened.

This was not merely a priceless object. There was something extraordinary about it, a wondrous enchantment. And nobody knew but him. The secret knowledge made him smile.

Early the next morning, as Parley prepared to depart, Bert ran downstairs with his letter tucked in the sleeve of his shirt. He waited around the corner of the keep until Parley was on his horse and his uncle had stepped back inside The Crags. Then he ran up to say good-bye.

Parley's eyebrows went up as he saw Bert coming. "Well, at least somebody looks like they slept well. You look ready to take on a host of Dwergh all by yourself!"

"Good morning, trusted courier," Bert said with a broad smile. He slipped the letter into Parley's bag, shielding it as best he could with his body. "Remember, this goes straight to Will. Not to my father or mother. And don't you read it, either. I sealed it, you know!"

Parley put his hand over his heart and grinned impishly. "I will deliver it only unto your brother's hands, my liege. And woe to anyone who stands in my way."

"You're such a fool, Parley. That's what we like about you."

"Stay out of trouble, now—if that's possible for you!" That was the last thing Parley said to him. Bert watched the courier ride off, and when he turned around he was not terribly surprised to see his uncle in the doorway.

Bert crafted his most angelic expression: mouth pursed

in a tiny smile, bright eyes blinking. "Good morning, Uncle!"

Hugh Charmaigne stepped out to block his path. "I told you to give your letters to me and that I would give them to the courier."

"I didn't want to trouble you, Uncle."

"That is a lie. You disobeyed me, because you do not trust me. I suppose you thought that I would read them first."

"It's not that—"

"Don't contradict me, whelp," Uncle Hugh snapped. "Your father doesn't rule here. I do. That means you don't question my orders, you just follow them. And when you disobey, I will punish you. You can depend on that. Now get to your room and stay there. I forbid you to come out until tomorrow."

"Yes, Uncle." Bert lowered his head and frowned. But what he really wanted to do was smile.

CHAPTER
14

Parley allowed his horse to slow its pace, because he was near a spot he'd always liked, just before the Cliff Road, when the valley began to fall away. A brook came down from the forest slope on the right, disappeared under heavy wooden planks on the road, and then spilled over a ledge and vanished into a mist. The watery sound was better than music to his ears. He wondered how anyone could just trot by a scene like this without pausing to appreciate it. Too many people spent their lives rushing about, worrying about things that didn't matter. That was their problem.

It was funny how people who saw Parley's missing eye, withered arm, and awkward gait always pitied him. If only you'd had better luck in battle, they'd say, you might even be a knight by now. No, Parley would say, don't feel sorry for me. What could be better than traveling around the barony, bringing news to lords and ladies, and making friends in every village? And who was to scold him if he took a little extra time along the way? If a lame arm, a limp, and a useless hole in his head were the price to pay for such a life, he considered it a bargain. Why, he was the baron's messenger, and everyone was glad to see him coming.

Among those glad to see Parley was a certain widow in a town that he'd pass through tomorrow. She had a face like a stale dumpling, but good heavens, the woman could cook. He was thinking of her and enjoying the fine mist that settled on his upturned face when a movement by the side of the road caught his eye. It was a young doe.

The widow would appreciate a share of that meal. Parley's mouth watered as he considered the stew she might produce from the tender meat. With all the stealth he could muster, he slipped off his horse and tethered it to the nearest tree. The doe took a few steps toward the brook and pawed the ground with a delicate hoof. So far she was not alarmed.

Parley slipped his quiver over his shoulder and notched an arrow in his bow. He wasn't as close as he'd prefer—with only one good arm and a missing eye, he was hardly the most adroit of archers—so he crept slowly toward the doe. She raised her head, and her tail flicked up. Parley froze and held his breath. The doe bounded across the brook and disappeared into the brush. He sighed. Was it worth it? His stomach insisted it was.

The valley below was forbidden to anyone but Lord Charmaigne's hunters—a typical edict from that brute—but Parley decided the doe wasn't technically *in* the valley. *Not yet, anyway.* He followed her across the stream, picking his way carefully, and stepping on stones where he could to keep from making noise. Below him, the doe descended a slope. Farther below was a rocky pool where the brook splashed down after rushing over the ledge.

The mist was thicker here. The sound from the brook concealed his steps. And the wind was in his face as he followed. *Three good signs for hunting,* Parley thought.

His hope rose until he slipped on wet leaves. He lost his balance in an instant and tumbled down, flinging the bow and arrow aside to keep from impaling himself. As the world pinwheeled by, he saw the doe bound away. He rolled to a stop at the bottom of the slope and ended up in a seated position with his legs splayed.

The brook was directly in front of him. And on the sandy bank, he beheld the strangest thing he'd ever seen.

It was a sculpture of stone, a little taller than knee-high. In the shape of a man, more or less . . . or a cross between a man and a frog—wide mouth, without a nose, and with two bulging white gems for eyes. But most remarkable of all, it was *moving.* Parley shook his head and wondered if the fall had left him woozy. Yes, it was moving, all right. Its head turned to look at him— if those diamond eyes could see, anyway. The broad mouth opened a crack, and a thin stream of smoke came out.

It was so odd that it took a moment for something

else to capture Parley's attention. A pair of sturdy, leather boots stood unoccupied on the sandy bank. His gaze kept moving across a trail of clues. A little farther to the right, slung over a branch, there was a wide belt with an enormous silver buckle, studded with gemstones that glittered green, red, and blue. A little farther, there were large rocks near the water, and draped across them to dry were many layers of clothes. Undergarments. Drawers. A leather shirt. A hooded cloak. All of these were the colors of moss, bark, and stone, so that they practically blended into the wilderness.

Parley's aching head finally deduced that the owner of these garments must be bathing nearby. After another uneasy glance back at the stone creature, he looked toward the brook. And, in fact, there the owner was, looking as startled as Parley. He was stark naked, which would have been more embarrassing if not for the long, thick beard that fell nearly to his knees.

What a curious little man, Parley thought. But no—if the man was little, it was only in height. This fellow, standing in the brook with a wet cloth in one hand, was as wide and brawny as any of the baron's men. Parley was amused for a moment. And then he was afraid, because he saw how pale the man was. Pale as ash. Pale as a man who rarely saw the light of day . . . because he spent most of his life under the ground . . .

"You—you're *Dwergh!*" he sputtered.

The Dwergh put up one hand. "Do not move. You cannot leave." The voice was low and gruff, as if a bear had learned to speak, and the accent was strange.

Parley disregarded the command and scrambled to his feet. He took just two awkward steps before an ax with an enormous blade whooshed past his face. It splintered with astonishing violence into the bark of the tree next to him. The handle stuck out horizontally in his path, bringing the courier to a sudden stop.

Parley knew the Dwergh in the brook had no place to conceal an ax, unless he had it tucked away in that great beard of his. So there was at least one more of the accursed beings here. And hadn't he heard that they always travel in bands? He looked back up the slope that he'd tumbled down, and through the mist he saw the dim outlines of more of those short, heavily built folk, blocking his way.

The gruff voice burst out again, calling strange words, "Mokh! *Gonchukh!*" Parley turned and ran, but he felt something heavy seize his leg with terrible strength, and he hit the ground with a thud. Whatever grabbed him felt *hot*—almost painfully so, even through the fabric of his pants. He looked down and saw the stone creature with its arms clamped around his leg below the knee. It squeezed until Parley cried out in pain.

You're done for, Parley, he told himself. He heard footsteps coming nearer. The Dwergh called to one another in more harsh words that made no sense.

So it was more than a rumor. After so many years the Dwergh, the enemies of the baron and the king, had returned. *And what will become of the baron's messenger now?* Parley thought. *All because of a doe . . .*

15

Bert stared at his reflection. *It must be almost dawn,* he thought. But he didn't feel tired. Somehow, sitting before the mirror and listening to its mysterious, tranquil breathing was better than sleep.

Besides, he had so much to think about. His father's last words to him were still on his mind. Even his brother's note troubled him. His brother, training under the great knight who was supposed to teach *him* to fight.

"It isn't fair," he said aloud.

The words came back in an echo. *Isn't fair.*

It isn't right, he thought.

And he heard another echo. *Isn't right.*

Bert seized the arms of the Witch-Queen's throne. A strange thing just happened: There was an echo to words he never said aloud. And he was suddenly, acutely aware that something was different. Something was *missing.*

He stared at the mirror. "You're not breathing anymore," he said.

And he heard the words again, like a whisper down a long corridor. *Isn't fair.*

Bert leaped out of his seat. He stood frozen until his

hands began to shake. Then he bolted—out of the cavern, into the Tunnel of Stars, and up the forty-nine steps. He pushed the secret door shut, leaped into his bed, and lay quivering with the blankets pulled over his head.

A few hours later, Aunt Elaine knocked on his door and invited him to ride with her into the valley. Bert agreed. But while he rode he thought only about the mirror and wondered if what he'd heard—that disembodied whisper—was only a dream.

"Are you sure it's all right for us to be out here?" he called ahead to his aunt.

"Why wouldn't it be?" said Aunt Elaine, turning around on her horse with a quizzical look.

"In case there are any . . . enemies or something."

"I have combed this valley for plants for many years, Bert. There are no enemies here."

Bert sighed. He'd hoped for some kind of clash at The Crags while he was there. He wondered if he'd ever see a true battle.

A sudden chill coursed through his body. His hands twitched on his reins. He was filled with an urge to turn the horse around and spur it to a frothing gallop all the way back to The Crags, so he could sit before the mirror again. The fright had worn off, and his curiosity returned, stronger than ever.

"We're almost there," Aunt Elaine called back. "To the place I wanted to show you."

"What is it?" Bert shook his shoulders, trying to shrug off the feeling.

"You'll see."

A wide, curving cliff loomed ahead of them, embracing a small forest of birch. They rode toward it, down an overgrown path, pushing aside white branches that groped from either side. In a tiny meadow just ahead, Bert spotted a low cottage made of stone. As they drew near, a fox darted out of the open door and fled into the brush. *Deserted*, Bert thought. His aunt pulled back on her reins, and Bert stopped beside her.

"This is where Snow White found sanctuary," she said.

"This cottage? The Dwergh lived *here*?" Bert asked quietly.

Aunt Elaine nodded. "They would have lived in their mines if it was up to them. But it was part of the agreement that Rohesia struck with them during the truce one hundred years ago. The Dwergh could mine these hills, but only if they granted her people an equal share of what they found. And she said they must live above the ground, where their numbers could be counted."

"The better to keep an eye on them," Bert said. He stared at the building of stone, still intact after a century. It looked like a miniature version of the keep at The Crags. *The Dwergh are a loathsome bunch*, he thought, *but they sure know how to work with rock.*

Aunt Elaine slid down the side of her horse. "You don't seem to like the Dwergh. Have you ever met one?"

Bert dismounted. "No. And I don't mean to, except in battle."

"Is that so?" Aunt Elaine said. She tethered her horse to the branch of a tree, and Bert did likewise. "Do you know why the truce with the Dwergh was broken, and the fighting began?"

"The Dwergh cheated us. They kept more than their share."

Aunt Elaine knelt beside a small, leafy bush. She pulled a trowel out of the pouch at her waist and pierced the soil around the plant. "Actually it was the king who changed the terms of the bargain. He demanded two-thirds of the precious ores and gems that the Dwergh uncovered."

"Well, they were on our land," Bert said.

"It wasn't that simple, Bert. It never is. The borders shifted many times during the centuries. But at any rate, the Dwergh were too proud to agree to the king's command."

"Too greedy, you mean."

Aunt Elaine gave him a sideways glance, then kept digging. "Their greed has been exaggerated, Nephew. Their pride has not." She put the trowel aside and plunged her hands into the dirt. "But you can blame both sides for the blood that spilled after that. The Dwergh were too quick to wield their axes, the men too eager to swing their swords. Both sides made terrible mistakes. Still, most of the things you've heard about the Dwergh have been overstated. They're not monsters, Bert." With a gentle tug, she lifted the plant from the ground. "Would you hold this for me?"

Bert cupped his hands to accept the plant. "You sound like you're fond of the enemy, Aunt Elaine."

Aunt Elaine wiped her hands with her apron. "Understanding the enemy's point of view doesn't make me the enemy, Bert."

Bert shrugged. A pleasant aroma reached his nose—sweet and minty. He brought the plant up for a closer sniff. "What is this?"

"Melissa," Aunt Elaine replied. She pulled a cloth from her pouch and doused it with water she'd brought with her. Then she took the plant from Bert and wrapped the wet cloth around its roots.

"Is it a cure for something?" Bert asked.

She stuffed the plant into a sack and nodded. "Melancholy."

16

Parley sat in the little stone room—a space with just three walls, more like a deadend or alcove in the mine where the Dwergh had brought him. *Alcove*, he thought, liking the sound of that better. He fiddled with the band of iron that was clamped to his leg. *Well, that's not coming off.* The other end of the chain was held by that odd, moving statue. Parley figured out what it called to mind: a gargoyle without wings. It sat there, nearly motionless. An occasional wisp of smoke escaped its mouth, and its diamond eyes glittered with inner light.

The courier slumped against the wall and stared at the stone ceiling, just five feet high. He wondered if it was day or night aboveground. Next to him on a little wooden table there was a mug filled with some kind of cider—delicious, he had to admit as he took another sip—and the dish he'd scraped clean. A broth studded with mushrooms and meat, not bad at all.

He heard heavy steps approaching. One of the Dwergh appeared around the corner. He had a small iron bucket in one hand, and in the other, the courier's bag that Parley had left with his horse. Parley caught a glimpse of the

Dwergh's profile as he turned. Like all those folk, his fore-head sloped down and blended seamlessly into his craggy nose with only a shaggy brow to mark the spot where forehead ended and nose began. This one seemed younger than the rest. But like the others, he resembled a brawny, full-grown man squished down to a height of no more than four feet. The Dwergh wore a leather vest. His enormous arms looked capable of pulling a tree out of the ground. There were wide bands of silver on his wrists, and thick rings on every finger.

The Dwergh tossed the bag onto the ground next to Parley, sending up a plume of dust. "We have decided you can have this back," the Dwergh said in his rum-bling, throaty voice. The accent was odd. It sounded as if he'd said, "Vee haff decided you kon haff thiss bock."

"Splendid. And now you'll let me go?"

"We will not," said the Dwergh. He brushed his beard with one hand, and dust and pebbles trickled out. "But it could be worse for you. Three of our seven think it is dangerous to let you live, because you might escape and reveal us."

Parley gulped, and smiled crookedly. *Three of our seven.* He worked out the math on his fingers. "Please thank the other four for me, will you, friend? And might you be among the majority?"

The Dwergh bowed. A short but formal bow with his eyes shut and his hands by his sides.

Parley opened his bag. Everything appeared to be

there, including the letter from Bert to Will, with its wax seal unbroken. He took the mug, raised it to the Dwergh, and guzzled. Then he wiped his mouth with his sleeve. "What's your name, friend?"

"I am Harth," said the Dwergh.

"Parley here. So what will become of me, Harth?"

Harth folded his arms across his beard and stared out from under the deep bushy ledge that was his brow. His eyes were beetle-black in a face as pale as bone. "You will be our prisoner. Until our work is done. Then we debate. Whether it is safe to let you go."

Parley decided for the moment to ignore the question of his fate, and what would happen if it wasn't safe to release him. "Your work, you say? What kind of work? Mining for silver? Gold? Gemstones?"

The Dwergh scowled. "We are not here for those things. Not this time. But that is not for me to say or you to know."

Parley raised his palms. "Fine, fine," he said. "I'm in no position to argue. Just promise me—when you debate my fate, let me have my say?"

Harth gave another bow, deeper this time. He walked over to the stone creature that held Parley's chain. "*Orth, Mokh,*" the Dwergh said. The thing tilted its head back and opened its mouth, revealing a wide throat that was blackened like the inside of a chimney. Harth used a pair of tongs to lift glowing coals out of the bucket and deposit them into the sooty throat. When five coals had been dropped in, the creature closed its mouth again. The three-fingered hand that wasn't holding the chain rested contentedly on its round, stone belly.

Parley gawked. "Um . . . that's interesting. What do you call that thing, anyway?"

"A molton," the Dwergh said. "Its name is Mokh. I will leave you now. Was the food good?"

"Very," Parley said. "What was it?"

"Your horse."

17

Bert paused at the bottom of the Tunnel of Stars. The flame of his candle danced as his hand shook. He blinked hard, took a deep breath, and stepped into the chamber. Before him, the mirror gleamed by the light of the flame.

"You spoke to me," he said.

He heard nothing for several moments. And then that whispery voice came, like the wind blowing through reeds: *Spoke to you.*

Bert swallowed hard and stepped closer. It hadn't been his imagination. The mirror could talk.

"How?" he said. "How is this possible?"

Once again there was a long, soundless pause. Bert cased into the chair and put the candle on the small table by its side. He stared at the mirror, waiting.

Tell me, the mirror said. The whisper was just loud enough for Bert to perceive. And there was something else about it; a kind of drowsiness. Like someone waking from a deep sleep, which Bert supposed it was.

When the mirror spoke, its skin of glass appeared to swirl. Ripples spread from the center and vanished under the golden frame. Bert looked into his reflection, pure and perfect as always, but it looked like something floated behind it—another face, not his own—deep inside the glass. For a moment it looked as if it might come to the surface, so that Bert could see it. Then it faded. Bert had the urge to run and hide in his bed again. He dug his fingernails into the arms of the throne, fighting the instinct.

Tell me, the mirror said again. Insistent.

Bert's voice cracked when he replied. "Tell you what?"

What troubles you.

Bert leaned back. He stared wide-eyed for so long that he had to remind himself to blink. "Nothing," he mumbled. "Nothing troubles me." A strange sensation came over him—the feeling that something was inside his skull, prodding and poking as if rummaging through a cluttered drawer. It didn't hurt. But it made him so dizzy he nearly pitched forward out of the chair. He lowered his head and closed his eyes, waiting for the feeling to pass. And it finally did. He raised his head again and stared at the mirror through the strands of coal-black hair that fell across his eyes.

You are angry, the mirror said. Its surface rippled again.

It suddenly occurred to Bert that his discovery of this magical thing was no accident. He hadn't stumbled upon it—fate steered him to it. And he knew why. Because he needed it. The mirror was meant to be his friend. He could talk to it, open his heart to it. "Well, of course I'm angry," he said.

Tell me, whispered the mirror.

"It's everything," Bert said. Every feeling that he'd kept inside spilled out as if a stopper was pulled. Hot tears welled in his eyes and tumbled down his cheeks. He wiped them with the cuff of his sleeve as he spoke. "I only came to The Crags because my brother Will was afraid, and now I feel like I've been banished. I did it to help him, but instead he's getting the lessons in fighting from this great knight, Andreas. Those lessons were meant for *me*! And it turns out that Father thinks Will might be the better baron anyway—that's the worst of it. So where does that leave me? Here, where everyone hates me. My uncle looks at me likes he wishes I was dead, because he despises my father so much. And his men won't look at me at all. The only one who can stand me is Aunt Elaine."

I don't hate you, Bertram.

Bert held his breath for a moment. Had he ever told the mirror his name? He couldn't remember. But it didn't matter. The mirror was his friend. He smiled. "Finding you was the only good thing that's happened to me here."

Yes, it is well that you found me. I will help you, the mirror whispered.

The candle on the table flickered. Bert shrank back in the chair. A cold shiver ran down his arms, frosting his flesh with goose bumps. "Help me? Help me do what?"

Have what you desire, the mirror whispered. *Live what you dream.*

"But . . . how do you know what I desire?" Bert felt that feeling again—something slithering and bumping along the folds and creases of his brain. Probing. His eyes lost focus. He said again, "How do you know?" His words were slurred. His eyelids fluttered and closed.

When they opened again, the candle he'd brought with him had gone out. He reached for it and felt only a hard puddle of wax and the charred stub of the wick. It was so dark it didn't matter if his eyes were open or shut. All he could see was a pale oval—the mirror glowing, though it had no light to reflect.

"Mirror?" he said.

Yes, my friend? the whisper came.

Bert edged toward where he thought the Tunnel of Stars might be, groping at dark air. "I've been down here too long. It might be morning. I have to go before someone knows I'm missing. I don't want this place discovered. I don't want *you* discovered."

Come back to me soon, Bertram.

"I will. Of course I will." He touched the wall on the far side of the cave and slid his hands across it until he found the threshold of the Tunnel of Stars. Then he went up the stairs, leaning forward and using his hands as well as his feet to climb. As he drew near the top, he saw a splinter of light where he'd left the secret door slightly open with a pebble to keep it from shutting entirely. He'd been afraid to let it close, in case he couldn't open it again and was trapped in the cave forever.

At the top of the steps, he eased the door open as little as necessary and squeezed out. He slid sideways with his back to the wall and emerged from behind the tapestry. He'd taken only a few steps across the floor when Uncle Hugh burst into the room.

There was a flash of surprise on his uncle's face—the shaggy eyebrows jumped and fell. Then the customary scowl returned, with the lip twitching on one side. "What? How did you get back in here! Where were you last night?"

At any other moment Bert would have quailed under that menacing glare. But he felt strangely calm, even as a pair of his uncle's savage-looking dogs padded into the room and stared at him with their snouts peeled back over their yellow teeth. Bert folded his arms and stared with mild disgust at his uncle. "I took a walk. Did I break one of your rules?"

Uncle Hugh stepped toward him with his right hand squeezed into a fist. Bert heard knuckles cracking.

"Father wouldn't like it if you hit me," Bert said coolly. He was amazed by his own composure.

Parts of his uncle's face went purple. "Sneaking around the castle at night, are you? Poking your nose into places it doesn't belong?"

Bert caught a whiff of sour breath. He wanted to laugh at this petty, pathetic man. "Why does that make you so mad? Do you have something to hide?"

Hugh Charmaigne sputtered. His fists trembled at

his sides. "That's it for you, boy. I'm bolting your door. And I'll find out what you're up to. I promise you that. And when I do I'll . . ." He didn't bother to complete the thought. He whirled around and left the room, followed closely by his dogs. When he slammed the door it was like a crack of thunder.

Bert walked to his bed and flopped on his back. He chuckled, feeling vastly pleased with himself. Confined to his room again! If only his uncle knew.

Something on the table by his bed caught his eye. It hadn't been there the day before. It was a bushy plant in a ceramic pot—the melissa that his aunt found near the Dwergh cottage. What was it for? *Melancholy*, she'd said.

Bert laughed again. He'd never felt less melancholy in his life. Something had happened to him while he slept before the mirror. A transformation. He felt strong. Exhilarated. Powerful.

Yes. Especially that. *Powerful.*

CHAPTER
18

"What do you mean, you're too sore?" Andreas folded his arms and stared down at Will.

"My legs are killing me," Will said, kneading one thigh with both hands. He was on a bench in a shaded spot in the courtyard, out of the hot sun. "And I can't even lift my arms." He raised one arm shoulder-high and winced, just to prove the point.

Andreas flicked his beard with his fingers. "Is that all that troubles you?"

Will turned away from Andreas's piercing stare. He wondered how the knight could tell. There was an epic list of things troubling him—starting with losing Bert—but these last few days, a fresh concern had been heaped atop the rest. "I'm worried about Parley. It's been a week, and he never came back from The Crags."

Andreas nodded. "I heard. But the men say this Parley often takes his time on the way back. Visiting . . . er, acquaintances."

Will shook his head. "Never this long. And not when there's something important to deliver." *Like a letter from*

109

Bert, he added inwardly. "Father sent another courier that way. Maybe we'll hear something soon."

"I'm sure you will," said Andreas. "In the meantime, since you are not prepared for the physical side of battle, we will discuss the intellectual side. I trust your brain is not sore as well?"

"No," Will said. One corner of his mouth turned up. "That's the only part that doesn't hurt."

Andreas squinted into the sunlight. He pointed. "That tower. Can you lead me there?"

Will followed his gaze, and his little smile faded. Andreas meant the lonely tower where he and Bert had spent so many hours. He'd never taken anyone else there before. It was a private spot for him and Bert alone. But he couldn't think of a reason to say no. "You mean now?"

"Of course," said the knight.

Will trudged across the courtyard with Andreas ambling behind. The aching muscles in his arms and legs loosened a bit as he climbed the narrow, winding stairs, but he decided not to mention that to the knight, so he didn't end up in the pads and helmet again.

"Why do the stairs curve this way?" Andreas said from behind him.

"Excuse me?" Will asked, puzzled.

"Why are tower stairs made to curve to the right as we ascend? Why not to the left?"

Will realized he was being tested. "I always figured it was to give the defender the advantage. The defender will be upstairs from the attacker. If he's right-handed, the defender has room to swing his sword. The attacker doesn't. And most folk are right-handed."

"Hmm," was all Andreas said.

They arrived at the tower. Will felt a tug in his heart. This was a place where he'd rarely been to without Bert by his side. Many devious plots had been hatched here. It was an incubator for mischief.

He watched Andreas walk the small round space with his hands clasped behind his back. The knight's keen eyes darted about, catching the fine details that Will had forgotten were there: pictures scrawled in charcoal on the walls, clay marbles in a circle of sand, apple seeds spat on the floor, wooden toys on the windowsills.

Andreas had his back to Will. "This is a hideaway. A special place."

Will's head shrank between his shoulders. "I suppose."

"I had one myself long ago. In the loft of a barn. Whiled away many happy hours there." Andreas sighed. "You didn't have to bring me here, you know."

"It's all right."

Andreas gave Will a jerk of the head that said "come here." "Well, then. Look out there and tell me: If you were to lay siege to Ambercrest, how would you do it?"

Will stepped up beside him. He didn't have to look, really. He knew every feature of the view from that window: outer walls, farms and fields, land that sloped away from the great mound in every direction, roads cast to the four points of the compass. "I would try to find some other way to win. Anything but a siege."

Andreas lifted an eyebrow. "Is that so?"

"A siege is the last resort. I'd try to lure them out first."

"Lure them out? How?"

"I don't know. If it was my father, I'd shout insults at him. He'd charge out soon enough. Then I'd pretend to run, and draw him away from his castle, to a better place to fight."

A crafty smile came to Andreas's face. He put one elbow to the wall and leaned on it. "Interesting. But what is so bad about a siege?"

Will rubbed his aching neck. "I suppose you have to do it, sometimes. But it's such a waste. I mean, the whole point of a castle like this is defense. You'd probably lose a third of your men before you even took the walls."

"And is that the only thing that matters? Caring how many men die under your command?"

Will squeezed his eyes half shut. "Well, sure. It matters a lot. But that's what's so awful about war. If you care too much about your men, you'll lose. That's one of the five great faults of a commander."

Andreas stiffened. "*What* did you say?"

Will's face warmed. Had he said something wrong? "Well, I read that there are five big faults a commander can have. One is caring too much about his men. Another one is a bad temper—you know, someone who can be provoked. Another is recklessness. Another is—"

"Where?" said Andreas, looming over him. There was a hungry look in his eyes. "You read this *where?*"

"I found some papers in our library," Will stammered, taking a half step back. "They're translated from something written a long time ago in some place far away. About war and how to wage it. It's not complete, though . . . and some of it's hard to understand. . . ."

Andreas pressed one palm against his forehead. "The words of the general of the east. In this godforsaken place." Those words were directed at the heavens, the next ones at Will. "How many pages? How many are there?"

"Thirty-five, I think. They're in the keep. Would you like to see them?"

The knight chuckled softly. "If you can't run all the way there, I'll carry you."

Andreas placed the final tattered page gently on the stack. He leaned back in the chair and let out a deep breath, like a man at the end of a feast. "The illuminated mind," he said. "How it shines, even through the fog of a clumsy translation."

"Father says it's mostly nonsense," said Will.

"Nonsense?" Andreas smirked and shook his head. He looked at the pile of parchment as if it was a beloved pet. "These are falling apart. I'll have to make a copy."

"Where did it come from?" Will asked.

"Some place far from here. An unknown kingdom. And it was written long ago. I've seen a scrap of the original language, in the king's archives. It doesn't even look like words, Will—just slashes of ink on the pages. Like little pictures."

"Is it Dwergh?"

Andreas shook his head. "No, it comes from farther away than that. From a land you could never hope to reach. At the far end of the world, with an endless desert and a thousand barbaric tribes between us."

"Then how did it get here?"

"By some miracle. Passed from one wanderer to the next, perhaps. Who knows? But you see the wisdom in these pages, don't you?"

Will shrugged. "In the parts I can understand."

"Then you're not the boy your father thinks you are," said Andreas. He rubbed his earlobe between two fingers, thinking. Then he leaned forward and spoke quietly. "Tell me something, Will. One day, your father will decide whether you or your brother will succeed him. Do you worry about that day—how things will go between you?"

"No," Will said. "Bert's my best friend, not just my brother. Besides, I know he'll be chosen. He's like my father. Brave and strong."

"But what if it was you, Will? What sort of baron do you think you'd be?"

Bert paced back and forth in his room, stopping when he heard a metallic scrape on the far side of his door. The bolt was sliding open. *Who is it now?* he wondered. He didn't want to talk to anyone. He just wanted them all to go to sleep. Then it would be safe to disappear through the wall and go to the mirror. *The mirror!* The thought of sitting before it again made him shiver with anticipation.

The door opened, and Aunt Elaine came in carrying a covered dish. She smiled. Bert tried to smile back.

"It must be hard for you," she said. She put the dish on the wooden table and sat in one of the chairs beside it. Bert slumped into the other seat.

"I've asked your uncle about letting you out again," his aunt said. "But he hasn't budged yet."

And I hope he doesn't. "Oh well," Bert said. He heard a creak and realized he was rocking back and forth in his chair. He grabbed the seat to make himself stop.

"You poor thing," Aunt Elaine said. "You're going crazy in here, aren't you?"

I'll feel better if you just shut up and leave, Bert thought. He fought back a powerful urge to scream at her. Then he took a deep breath and leaned back in his chair. *Calm down, Bert. What's the matter with you? She's always been nice.*

"You must be hungry. Here's your dinner," said Aunt Elaine. She uncovered the dish. There was a bowl of soup, teeming with green leaves, and a fat slab of bread with a gob of half-melted butter. "I get the feeling you want to be alone, Bert. But haven't you had enough of solitude?"

Bert shrugged. "I really don't mind. I prefer it, in fact."

Aunt Elaine stared at him, frowning, for too long. "Is there anything else troubling you, Bert? This confinement is terrible enough, of course. But . . . you seem different somehow. Is there anything you want to tell me?" She reached out to pat his hand, but Bert jerked his arm away. Again he had to bite off an angry shout. It was infuriating, the way she seemed to look right into his mind.

"Why would I have anything to tell you? I'm fine, Aunt Elaine. I'll stay all summer in this room if I have to."

Aunt Elaine stood and smoothed the front of her dress. "All right, Bert. But I'll talk to your uncle again. Can I at least tell him you'll apologize for being rude?"

Bert ripped off a hunk of bread and popped it into his mouth. It had no flavor. "Tell him whatever you like," he said without looking at her. His aunt left, not saying another word. He heard the bolt snap back into place on the other side of the door.

Finally, Bert thought, exhaling loudly. He looked longingly at the tapestry that concealed the Tunnel of

Stars. He wanted badly to run down those stairs, right away. But he knew it wasn't safe. He had to wait until everyone else had gone to bed. Two hours? Three? The minutes would feel like years.

At least, with the door bolted shut, he figured his uncle wouldn't bother to check on him. As far as Lord Charmaigne knew, Bert had no way out.

He closed his eyes, hugged himself with his arms crossed, and rocked back and forth in his chair, no longer caring about the noise it made. *Squeak. Squeak. Squeak. Squeak.*

"I'm here, Mirror," Bert said, running to the throne. He wiped the perspiration from his brow. His teeth hurt from clenching his jaw.

I am glad you are here. I have been thinking about you.

Bert settled into the chair. A surge of pride warmed his veins. *The mirror was thinking about me!* "You have? What have you been thinking?"

How you must miss your brother.

Bert leaned to one side and rested his chin on one hand. *My brother.* In truth, he'd been feeling something toward Will that he'd never felt before. Resentment. Jealousy. It grew by the hour, consuming his thoughts.

Would you like to know what he is doing? the mirror whispered.

"What he's doing? Sleeping, probably," said Bert, lifting his head from his palm.

I can tell you what he is doing.

"Tell me? How?"

You must ask.

"Ask?" Bert's brow furrowed. He straightened from his slouch and gripped the arms of the chair. "You mean, like 'Tell me what Will is doing'?"

The mirror flickered, like lightning inside a distant cloud. Its surface took on that liquid appearance again. Ripples started from the center and disappeared under the frame. There was a humming, whining sound, like a moistened finger circling the rim of a crystal goblet.

The mirror spoke.

The hour is late. Most in Ambercrest are sleeping. But a man and a boy talk deep into the night, in a room filled with papers, lit by candles. They discuss the philosophy of war, the art of leadership. The man is a knight. The boy is your brother. The knight asks Will what sort of baron he would be. Will says he would be fair and honest, slow to anger . . .

"Enough!" cried Bert. He shot out of the chair and stomped about the chamber, clutching a handful of hair. "What's Will talking about? He always said I'd be the one, not him! That should be *me*! I should be getting those lessons, not Will! Why didn't Father just send Andreas back to wherever he came from when he found out I'd left?" He walked to the side of the chamber and bashed the wall with his fist. "Why is this happening?" he muttered. He remembered again what Father had said when he leaned into the carriage with that conspiratorial gleam in his eye, thinking Bert was Will. *I know everyone believes that Bert will be baron one day. But I wouldn't assume that if I were you.* And now Will was telling the knight what a great baron he'd be.

"Perfect," Bert said in a voice like acid. He put his forehead on the cold stone. "Just perfect. Father must have been so happy that I switched places with Will. It worked out just right for both of them, didn't it?"

Don't lose hope, Bert, the mirror whispered. *You may still get what you desire.*

"No," Bert said. "I'm losing everything. I'll never get what I want."

You will get what you desire. If you let me help you. If you use me.

Bert lifted his head and turned around to look at the mirror. "Use you?" A dark thought shadowed his mind. "Wait. Did the Witch-Queen use you?"

I do not know that name, said the mirror.

"Rohesia. This was her secret place. She must have used you to see things too. The way you told me what Will was doing. Didn't she?"

Ah, Rohesia. A dark time, said the mirror. *Rohesia was vain. She was mad. She was not like you. She was born to relish her own beauty and envy those around her. She used me for wicked purposes, but you will not. She was weak, but you are strong. You were born to be a great leader, Bertram. A mighty ruler of men. A barony is not enough for you. Nor even a single kingdom.*

"Yes," said Bert. He could feel the truth of the words. His heart pounded like a gong of war. "I *was* born for that. I feel it."

But a rival plots to take this from you. To steal your birthright.

"What?" Bert raised his chin and quivered with anger. "Who plots against me? *Who?*"

You already know, the mirror said. *The truth is plain to see, but you don't wish to recognize it.*

Bert lifted his hands. They were shaking. "Not . . . my brother?"

And now you understand. He tricked you into taking his place.

"But Will is . . . He wouldn't . . ." Bert gasped. That strange feeling was back, stronger than before; something prodding and poking inside his mind. He thought about his brother, talking with the knight about war. Leadership. Being baron. And his blood steamed with rage. "It's true, isn't it? Will wanted me out of the way."

He wanted you to believe he was afraid to leave. But that was a lie.

"Yes. Of course it was a lie. And now this great teacher is giving him the lessons that were meant for me."

Lessons he will use against you.

"Against me!" Bert snapped. It was so obvious. How could he have been fooled so easily? All his life Will had lied to him. And yet . . . a small voice in his head cried out as if from a vast distance. *It can't be true,* the voice said. *Will is my brother. He loves me.*

Bert groaned and pressed his fingers against his temples. Again he felt something moving inside his skull, like fingers in his brain. But it wasn't gently prodding now. It twisted and shoved and squeezed. The little voice that had piped up let out a strangled cry, and then fell silent. Bert closed his eyes and saw white sparks against his lids. He lurched and seized the back of the Witch-Queen's throne to keep from falling. Finally the strange probing ended. Had a minute passed? An hour? He couldn't tell. He opened his eyes and blinked hard.

It was clear to him now, perfectly clear. The veil was torn away, the treachery revealed. He could feel it. He knew it. The wonderful mirror had helped him understand.

"Something must be done about my brother." His voice rang out strong and echoed off the walls. "But what?"

I will help you, the mirror said.

There was a sound, low and rumbling. At first Bert thought it might be a boom of thunder, with the noise sifting down through the tiny crevices in the ceiling. But as the noise grew he realized it was stone grinding against stone.

A crack appeared in the wall beside the mirror, and widened. Bert's jaw slackened as he watched the wall of stone swing open. A second chamber, much larger than the first, was revealed. Bert's candles cast a band of yellow light into the dark, new space, a band that grew wider as the wall continued to open.

The first thing Bert saw was a cauldron, squatting on three stubby legs over a circle of stones filled with ancient ashes.

Then shelves filled with pots and vessels and jars.

Then a chest-high table holding an enormous book and stacks of parchments.

Then tall, narrow boxes, big enough to stand inside, but not wide enough to sit.

Get away, the little voice in Bert's mind called out from a mile away. *This is a bad place.* Bert felt a pinch in his brain and a wet crunch—two fingers squeezing something between them—and the voice was gone.

"I . . . can't believe it," Bert said. He took a candlestick and walked into the new chamber. A papery flutter passed his ear. He looked up to see a bat with its jagged wings flapping madly by. It flew to the far end of the chamber and disappeared through a gap in the wall.

Another way out, Bert thought. *I wonder where it leads?*

A secret exit, the mirror said behind him, *so you may leave unseen if you wish.*

Bert walked to the cauldron. It was so big that his arms would only go halfway around, if he hugged it. Inside, it was empty, except for the frail skeleton of a rat that must have fallen in and gotten trapped.

There was a pile of wood behind the cauldron. It collapsed under the weight of his foot when he prodded it, rotted away after a hundred years. Next to the useless wood was a heap of shiny coal.

He turned to look at the tall boxes. Each one had a latch and a slit near the top, where the eyes would be if someone was locked inside. Where the flickering candle-light pierced the gloom of that tiny opening, he caught a glimpse of something pale and smooth, yellow-white.

Turning away from that grim sight, he walked to the table. His gaze landed on the tall stacks of parchment next to the ancient-looking book. The papers were covered with hand-written notes. He looked through a few of them: "I have come to doubt the use of horehound to cure a wicked cough" . . . "Costmary may drive moths from a place" . . . "A woman in the hills insisted that yarrow will heal the ghastliest wounds" . . .

Bert frowned as he realized what he'd found: The lost notes of Rohesia. The knowledge of healing that his aunt so desperately wanted. Well, he couldn't give them to her now, not without raising questions about where they were discovered. He dropped the pages back on the table. And then his heart nearly exploded as a gruff, triumphant voice rang out behind him.

"So this is where you've disappeared to!"

Bert's mind reeled as he watched Uncle Hugh step out of the Tunnel of Stars and into the chamber.

"Stupid boy," his uncle said. "Did you think I wouldn't find your secret? I went in to check on you. Then I heard a noise from behind the tapestry. What is this place?" Uncle Hugh's darting eyes settled on the mirror. He stared and swallowed like a starving man who'd seen a roasted pig set before him. "And what is *this*?" he said, walking toward the glass.

Bert didn't think. He just leaped between his uncle and the mirror. "Get away," he snapped. A fleck of spit flew from his mouth. "It's *mine!*"

Uncle Hugh's hand shot up, and his fingers clamped around Bert's face, covering it nearly from ear to ear. His uncle threw him aside, and Bert tumbled across the cavern floor. There was a stab of pain in his back as he rolled over a loose stone the size of a brick.

He looked up and saw his uncle in front of the mirror. Uncle Hugh's eyes went to the exquisite frame, and he brushed his fingers along the sculpted gold and silver. "Magnificent . . . worth more than all the treasure in

Ambercrest," Uncle Hugh said. "And right under my nose, all these years."

Bert snorted like a bull. He pushed himself to his knees. His hand brushed against the rock that he'd rolled over. And then he heard the voice of the mirror— not through his ears, but echoing in his mind: *Others plot to steal this from you, your birthright.*

"It's *mine*," Bert said. The words came out in a hiss.

Uncle Hugh didn't even turn to look at him. "Nonsense. Everything in this castle belongs to me. Everything." He put his face so close to the mirror that his nose touched it.

His ugly, oily nose, thought Bert. His fingers closed around the stone. He stood and crept slowly forward, careful to stay behind his uncle's broad back, out of sight of his reflection.

Uncle Hugh reached out and brushed the perfect glass with his fingertips. "So cold," he said. "Like ice!" He stared at his image, so engrossed that he never heard Bert come stealthily behind him.

Bert raised his hand and paused. *What am I doing?* he thought.

You will lose me if you don't, the mirror told him.

I can't, Bert thought. But the strangest thing happened. He watched his hand draw back and whip forward again, bringing the stone across the back of his uncle's head. Uncle Hugh groaned and threw his arms up. He sagged to his knees, then wobbled and fell to one side. He didn't move except for the twitching of one hand.

Bert's fingers loosened, and the stone thumped on the cavern floor. "What! How? I didn't do that! I didn't!" he cried.

It had to be done, the mirror said. *He would have taken me away.*

Bert's chest heaved, and he clenched his teeth. "No! Nobody can take you. You're mine."

There isn't much time, the mirror said. *Close the door before someone else finds it.*

"Yes—the door!" Bert grabbed his candle and ran to the tunnel and up the stairs. He saw a dull glow at the top. The secret door was wide open. He slid behind the tapestry to its edge and poked his head out. The door to the hallway was ajar, but nobody else was in the room. No *person*, anyway—three of his uncle's dogs were at the threshold. One of them saw Bert. The fur bristled on its back, and it showed its yellow teeth, but the dog did not come for him. It was afraid, just like the bird and the kitten had been.

Bert slipped back through the opening behind the tapestry. He heaved on the stone door and pushed it until it was nearly closed—his pebble would keep it from shutting completely. *Hurry*, the mirror whispered into his mind from afar. Bert moved down the stairs as fast as he could without falling.

Uncle Hugh was still on the floor. His fingers weren't

just twitching now. His hand rose, grasping something that wasn't there. He moaned.

"What do I do?" Bert said. His mouth had gone dry.

Listen carefully. On the shelves before you. Find the long-necked yellow bottle.

"Long-necked yellow bottle," Bert repeated as he ran into the new chamber. There were bottles of every color on the shelves. He found the container the mirror meant, one with a fat, round bottom and a slender neck. There was a cork pushed into the top and sealed with gobs of black wax. All the jars were sealed this way. He saw a dark liquid slosh inside and was surprised that it hadn't dried up after all these years. Bert looked at the single word etched on the front of the bottle: SOMNUS.

He ran back to the mirror. His eyes widened as he saw his uncle lift his head off the floor. Uncle Hugh's eyelids fluttered up, and his eyes tried to focus.

Open the bottle, the mirror said. Bert tore at the brittle wax, and it broke away in his hands. He tugged on the cork and couldn't budge it. So he clamped it between his teeth and pulled. The cork popped out.

Bert shuddered as a hand brushed against his leg. His uncle groped for him. Bert stepped back as the hand clutched at the air.

Touch the potion to his lips, the mirror said. Bert gulped. Uncle Hugh groaned, put his palms to the floor, and pushed, trying to raise himself. But one arm collapsed, and he rolled over onto his back, blinking away the pain.

Bert saw his chance. He darted in and tipped the bottle. Most of it vanished into Uncle Hugh's beard, but some went between his parted lips. A moment later his uncle's eyes closed again, and his breathing slowed. He was still.

He will sleep, the mirror said.

"For how long?" Bert asked.

Long enough to prepare the next potion. The essential potion. Now go to the book, Bert. You must find the spell called "The Slave of the Mind."

Bert felt tightness in his stomach, like a knot pulled from both ends. "You want me to cast a spell? But this sounds like . . . something Rohesia would have done."

Ah, but you are not doing this for evil, Bertram. You only do this because you must. If you don't, he will take me from you. Do you want that to happen?

"No, of course I don't. . . ."

And your dream, Bertram. To someday be baron. To be more than a baron. You want that, don't you?

"Of course."

Then heed me, Bertram.

And Bert knew that he would. He would heed the mirror. Because the mirror was wise.

The mirror was his friend.

"Par Lee." That was how the Dwergh said his name, as if it were two names instead of one.

"I came to see if you are well, Par Lee," Harth said.

"Bored out of my mind, but fine otherwise," Parley replied. He'd been lying on a straw mat that the Dwergh brought him. He sat up and crossed his legs. The chain at his ankle clinked, and he glanced at the Molton squatting nearby, motionless.

"What's this little fellow's name again?" Parley asked.

"Mokh," Harth said. The molton's stone head swiveled at the sound of its name.

"Mokh," Parley repeated. The molton turned toward him. Parley waggled his fingers, waving, but there was no response that he could detect in that glittering stare. *About as friendly as his masters,* he thought.

Harth started to walk away, but stopped when Parley called after him.

"Why seven?" Parley said.

"Eh?" said Harth.

"Why are there always seven of you? Is that some Dwergh tradition?"

Harth clasped his hands behind his back and thrust his chest forward. "Seven for the seven precious gems we seek. For the seven kings of old. For the seven great caverns in the seven great mountains. For the seven days of the week. Each of us in turn takes one day of rest. Today is my day."

"You seem pretty busy to me."

"And what would you do on a day of rest, Par Lee?"

"I'd lie about, talking nonsense."

"As you are doing right now?"

Parley opened his mouth to answer, than narrowed his eyes. There was a twinkle in Harth's eye. He was sure of it.

"Was that a joke?" Parley said, beginning to grin.

He saw, deep inside the Dwergh's thick beard, that Harth smiled too.

"I didn't know the Dwergh had a sense of humor. That was a good one, my friend," the courier said.

The smile faded from Harth's face. "Friend? You have called me that before. Why do you use that word, when we are sworn enemies?"

"I never swore such a thing," Parley said.

"Nor did I. It was your king, many years ago."

"Yes. Now that's the real nonsense. Someone really ought to do something about that."

"Some things break and cannot be fixed, Par Lee," said the Dwergh.

Parley shrugged. "And some things just take longer to mend." Somewhere deep in the mines he heard the incessant clang of picks on stone. It never stopped, day or night—not that he could tell one from the other in this hole in the Earth.

"What are you doing here, anyway?" he asked before Harth could walk away again.

Harth stared back keenly. "We look for something."

"Gems? Gold?"

Any hint of friendship left the Dwergh's face. "That is how you think of us, is it? Greedy folk in dark holes, wanting only to pry precious stones from the ground. We are more than that, Par Lee. We know that we are not welcome here, and that if we are discovered, we will be killed. I assure you, the task that calls us here is important. And what we do, we do for the sake of your people as well as ours."

Parley's hand had wandered up his chest like an insect, and rested at his throat. "What on Earth are you looking for?"

Harth hesitated. He glanced down the stone corridor, where the faint clanging could still be heard. "Something left behind long ago, Par Lee. A poison we must extract from this land. And we shall succeed, if that is the will of the earth." The Dwergh didn't wait for another question. He turned and strode down the tight stone passage, vanishing into the blackness.

Parley sighed. It was awfully dull sitting there with only a mute lump of animated stone for company. He stared at the molton. "How about a game of dice,

Mokh?" he said. The creature turned its diamond eyes toward him. "I'll keep score," Parley said with an encouraging smile. "Here's all you have to do. Look—seven dice! Excellent number, right?" He rolled the dice on the ground. "Ah, bad roll. I only matched a couple of threes. Here, you try it!" He scooped up the dice and offered them to the molton. Mokh looked down at the dice and up at Parley, expressionless as always. Then, as Parley watched with a mix of fascination and confusion, the molton scrunched its shoulders and bunched its three-fingered hands into fists. It trembled violently, and Parley swore he heard a grunt—the first sound he'd ever heard the strange being utter. The molton stood up from its squat, walked a few feet away with the chain dragging behind it, and sat again. Parley gaped at the spot it left, where a small pile of cold white ash had been deposited.

He glared at Mokh, almost certain he saw a hint of a grin on that mineral face. "Well, if that isn't the rudest thing ever! So that's what you think of my game, eh? See if I ask you to play again."

He slumped against the cold wall and sighed. *They won't have to execute me. I'll die of boredom first*, he thought. He looked down at his courier's bag. Inside was the note that Bert had written to Will. He picked up the parchment and eyed the wax seal. If he broke it and read the letter, could he fix the seal, so nobody would notice it had been opened? He felt himself turn red in the face. *Now, Parley*, he chided himself, *be a good courier. Tedium is no excuse for reading what was never meant for you.* Still it was tempting. And since he was unlikely to get out of this alive, would it really matter? *Yes, it matters,* he assured himself. *Right is right. And wrong is wrong.*

22

"Let's ride a little farther," Andreas said. "Do you think you can?"

Will opened his mouth to take a deep breath. He turned in his saddle and looked back at Ambercrest. The castle and its sprawling walls were so distant that he could hold the sight of them in his cupped hand.

"I think so," he said.

"Why don't you lead?" said Andreas.

Will nudged his horse with the heel of his boots, and the beast trotted along the road. This was Andreas's plan: ride a little farther each day along each of the four roads that led away from home. And it was working. The first time, Will felt his chest tighten as soon as they ventured beyond the farmlands surrounding the outer walls. But every day since, Will felt the boundaries of his comfort expanding. There was always an invisible barrier he'd reach, a place that made his legs quake and his mind go numb with fear. But with every sojourn, that border gave way. And it didn't just retreat—it weakened. Crumbled. Will had the idea that one day he might just be able to rush at it and leap over it and leave it behind for good.

But not yet.

He looked again at Ambercrest. Only its tallest spires were visible. And suddenly the panic seized him. He forgot how to breathe. A spike of pain pierced his chest, burning so hot that he pressed his palm against the spot. This was how it went: He'd think progress was made, that the worst was behind him, but the feeling would rush back.

"Is it the fear again?" Andreas said. The knight was somewhere behind him, but Will could only stare at the ground and nod with the reins clutched tight in his hands, concentrating on drawing air down his constricted throat.

"I remember the time in my life I was most frightened," Andreas said, stopping beside him. "I was sixteen years old, not yet a knight in the king's army. The Northmen had invaded as they still do from time to time. They are cruel, tall folk with thick shields and broad swords, ferocious in battle. We were encamped on a hill one night, and our sentries woke us with grim news: We'd been seen, and we were surrounded. I looked out and saw torches on all sides, closing in. Hundreds of them against just forty of us. The Northmen began to jeer and laugh, and they called out terrible threats."

There was a pause. Will lifted his head and looked at Andreas, who stared into the distance to the north and west, where Will supposed the battle must have taken place.

"There was nowhere to run," Andreas said. "Nothing to do but draw our swords and wait. I felt the way I suppose you do now—like the air itself was being robbed from my lungs, and my ribs might close like a fist around my heart and crush it. I was terrified, Will. Bug-eyed and shaking. Fear rushed down on me like a wave. Do you know what I did? I closed my eyes and let it wash over me. I let it happen. I let it pass. And then a curious thing happened: I found out what was on the other side of my fear."

Will looked up into Andreas's eyes. "What was there?"

"My courage."

"What do you wish of me?" said Uncle Hugh. There was a vacant look in his eyes as if he was lost in thought or not quite awake. He rarely blinked. And when he did, his lids fell and rose slowly.

Bert handed him a letter, rolled and sealed. "Send this to Ambercrest. In it, I suggest that my brother come to The Crags to visit." His lip curled into a sneer. "Because I miss him so."

"Yes, my nephew," Uncle Hugh said.

"But first I want you to add a letter of your own. Tell my parents what a good boy I've been. And how my conduct should be rewarded with a visit from my beloved brother."

Uncle Hugh lowered his head. "Of course, my nephew. It will be done."

"And then, after the letters are sent . . ."

Uncle Hugh had turned toward the stairs. He turned back again. "Yes, my nephew?"

A smile came to Bert's face, though his eyes blazed fiercely under slanted brows. "Bring me your dogs."

* * *

Bert heard his uncle curse and scream at the whining dogs. They didn't want to enter the Tunnel of Stars. Finally their hulking shadows appeared at the bottom of the stairs, and all eight of the enormous animals were prodded into the chamber, herded by a sweaty, panting Uncle Hugh. They cowered at his side, whining, with ears flattened and tails curled between their legs, looking as meek as puppies.

"Bring them here," Bert said. He pointed to the wide bowl at his feet, where raw chunks of meat soaked in a thick, yellow oil. His uncle shoved the dogs toward the bowl. They lowered their snouts and sniffed at the meat.

"Make them eat it," Bert said to Uncle Hugh.

"Eat," his uncle snapped, pointing.

There was a moment of hesitation. Then one dog eased its mouth open and gingerly clamped its teeth around a hunk of flesh. The others joined in. The sounds of chewing, smacking, and tearing filled the cool cavern air. Bert watched from his throne with two fingers pressed against his temple.

The dogs grew more ravenous as they ate, snarling as they fought for the last few pieces. When the meat was gone, they scraped the bowl clean with their tongues. Bert leaned forward and bounced a fist on the arm of his chair, thinking about his brother and trying to calm the rage that grew stronger by the minute.

One of the dogs started to growl, and soon the rest joined in. They paced in a circle around the empty bowl and snapped at phantoms in the air. Their mouths filled with gray foam that overflowed from their jaws and hung like beards. The growls turned into bubbling, gargling sounds. The dogs seemed to weaken. Their steps grew shorter, and their legs bent until their bellies scraped the ground as they slunk. Finally, almost as one, they fell onto their sides. Their chests heaved, their tongues spilled out onto the floor, and the foam pooled around their jaws.

"What's happening to my dogs?" Uncle Hugh asked dreamily.

"Wait and see," Bert said, leaning back in the throne. He rested his face on his hand and smiled. "Now tell me something, Uncle. Just because I'm curious, not because it matters anymore. Were you up to something, here at The Crags? Plotting against the baron? Thinking about setting up your own little kingdom, hmmm?"

Uncle Hugh's mouth twisted and shook as if he did not want to answer. His eyes watered, and he squeezed them shut. Finally, haltingly, he spoke as the words were forced out against his will. "Hated my brother . . . for being named baron instead of me . . . for ordering me to this pile of rock . . . dreamed about his death . . . gathering men, turning them against him . . . but I need more . . . biding my time . . ."

"Enough," Bert said, waving his hand. "You can forget all that now. There will be revenge, Uncle, but it won't be yours. And I won't bide my time, either." He looked at the dogs as they jerked and twitched amid a growing pool of spittle. Then he turned to the dark hole at the end of the chamber. "Now, Uncle, take a torch and find out where that passage leads to."

Behind Bert, the mirror flickered and glowed.

Parley heard footsteps approach the alcove. He opened his courier's bag and stuffed something inside before the approaching Dwergh turned the corner.

Harth appeared, and then Kholl, the ancient leader of the band of seven. Of all the pale, rough-hewn faces in the company, Kholl's was the grimmest. His eyes were set so far under his bushy brow that they seemed to peer out from a cave.

As far as Parley could tell, these were the only two of the seven Dwergh who could speak his language. "Hello, friends," he said, standing and brushing dust off his legs.

"How do you fare, Par Lee?" said Harth.

"It's the time of my life, Harth. Not bored at all. Mokh here is a delightful companion."

"I told you Par Lee was funny," Harth said out of the side of his mouth to Kholl.

"Tell him why we are here," replied Kholl, who didn't appear the least bit amused. Parley realized that this might be the moment he'd dreaded, when his fate was to be decided. Perhaps the Dwergh had already concluded that he must die to keep their secret.

It always amazed him how long a fateful moment could last. It was only a few seconds later that Harth spoke, but Parley had time to reflect that his had been a good life. He wished he'd made a few more friends, played a few more games, tasted a few more pies, seen a little more of the world. But when Harth finally spoke, it had nothing to do with his fate. Not yet, anyway.

"We want to show you something," the younger Dwergh said.

"Show me something?" Parley said. He cleared his throat. "By all means."

"We will unchain you, for now," Kholl said. "A man like you is no threat to escape. Not where we will take you."

Well, here's a little more of the world and not the part you expected, Parley told himself as Kholl led them on a long and strange subterranean journey, lighting the way with a silver lantern. Harth was behind him with a second light, and Mokh trotted along at the rear with a torch, taking five steps for every one of Parley's. They began in the kind of mine that Parley had always pictured—a dank, black corridor where heavy timbers propped up the loose earth overhead. Then they came to a place where the mine split into two passages—one tunnel that was ancient and the other one new, judging from the age of the wooden beams. From the new passage Parley heard the harsh song of tools on stone, the same sound that carried all the way to his alcove. Kholl turned the other way, toward the older passage. Parley hoped that the ceiling might be a little higher in this section, but it was the usual Dwergh height, and so he continued to stoop as he limped after Kholl.

"You have been injured many times in your life, Par Lee," Harth said from behind.

"Noticed the limp, eh?" Parley replied over his shoulder. "Well, all my injuries happened early in my sad career as a soldier. In my first battle, I lost an eye. In my second battle, because I was blind on one side, I didn't see some knave coming at me, and I got my leg skewered by a spear. In my third battle, because I couldn't dodge fast enough on my bad leg, I got my arm broken when a horse ran over me. As I was lying on the ground with hoofprints on my back, I decided to get out of the army business before I hurt something I really cared about."

Parley heard a low rumbling sound, and it was only when he noticed Kholl's shoulders shaking that he realized he'd gotten a laugh out of the craggy Dwergh. The courier grinned. *You'll call me friend yet, old-timer.*

They rested once, and Harth offered Parley water from a skin that he carried. Kholl did a strange thing. He called Mokh to him, and the molton trotted over with its torch held at arm's length. Kholl uncorked a little brass vessel and poured the oily contents over Mokh's head and shoulders. When that was done, the molton touched the torch to its head, and the oil burst into flames that engulfed the stone creature. Parley was alarmed at first

CATANESE

until he saw that Mokh was as content as Parley would
have been, basking on a sunlit rock. The molton even
folded its arms to allow all of its body to be enveloped by
flame, and stood that way until the fire had flickered out.
The joints of the creature's shoulders, elbows, wrists, and
fingers glowed red-hot.

Parley stared, fascinated, and something occurred to
him. "It needs the heat, doesn't it? That's why you feed it
coals."

"Of course," Harth said. "Without them the molton
would cease to move. Until someone warmed it again,
even a thousand years later."

They moved on, and soon the shaft ended in a wall of
solid rock with a jagged crack down the middle. Kholl
turned sideways and grunted as he squeezed his thick
chest through the crevice. Parley followed, and saw that
they'd passed into a cave that was sculpted by nature's
hand and not the pickaxes and hammers of the Dwergh.
The ceiling was lofty, and he was relieved to finally stand
straight without fear of knocking himself silly on a jutting rock or crossbeam. His one eye glimpsed enormous
carrots of stone, dangling overhead, like the fangs of a
giant beast.

As they walked on, Parley heard a roaring sound grow
in volume. Then he felt a different sensation under his
feet as they stepped onto a bridge made of wooden
planks and iron chains. It swayed with every step, and
Parley was grateful for the railing made of rough cord. In

the meager light, he saw white froth roiling by under the bridge. "A river under the earth. Who'd have believed such a thing?" he muttered.

The ceiling of rock curved into a solid wall on the other side of the river. Two natural columns of stone were there, strange formations that grew thin in the middle like titanic hourglasses. Between the two a perfect black rectangle was chiseled into the wall, leading to a dark, inner chamber. Harth stepped inside while Kholl stopped at the threshold and turned to face Parley. "None of your jokes now, Par Lee. This is a sacred place where your kind has never stepped. Only whispers here."

Parley looked into the stern face of the elder Dwergh. "Why have you allowed me here? What have I done to earn this?"

Kholl waved toward the chamber with a calloused hand. "Harth likes you. He wants you to understand us."

Parley coughed. He pulled on the hem of his shirt to straighten it and passed a hand over his thin hair to smooth it. He didn't know what to say, so he just stepped through the threshold into a small chamber.

It was round in shape, with a ceiling so low he had to crouch once again to keep from hitting his head. There were seven stone coffins inside with heavy slabs for lids. They were arranged in a circle with the ends nearly touching. Harth stood in the center holding his lantern high, like the yellow eye of a gray-petaled flower.

"These were her friends," Harth said.

Seven coffins! A thousand shivering dots of flesh erupted on Parley's arms. "*Her* friends? Emelina? Snow White?"

Harth closed his eyes and nodded. "We bury our folk near the mine that was closest to their hearts."

Parley limped forward, close enough to touch the nearest coffin. He was already stooping, so it was easy to drop to his knees. And it felt right. He kissed his fingers, put his hands on the stone slab, and lowered his head. "The seven that saved Snow White, buried here," he marveled.

"Not all seven. Not yet," Harth said.

Parley lifted his head and opened his good eye. He hadn't noticed at first, but one stone coffin was uncovered, with its lid propped against its side. He looked at Harth, questioning, and Harth jabbed his chin toward the entrance of the chamber.

Parley slowly turned. When his eyes found Kholl, the old Dwergh bowed.

"You . . ." Parley gasped. "One of Snow White's seven?"

"I was the youngest, by many a year," Kholl said.

"Good heavens, Kholl . . . You must be as old as the hills!"

Kholl thrust his chest forward. "One hundred and sixty-seven. And still strong enough to swing a pick."

Bert paced around the pack of dogs lying on the cold stone floor, twitching and senseless. Strange things were happening to them. It looked as though moles were burrowing just under the skin, leaving bulging tunnels in their wake. The shape of the dogs changed with every pass, growing thicker and more distorted.

And there were strange noises, muffled by skin and fur. Creaking, groaning, squishing, popping, and stretching. Through it all, the dogs whined and growled in their sleep, if they were sleeping at all. Their heads were lost inside the clouds of foam that streamed from their open jaws.

Bert knelt to examine the paws of the largest dog. Its feet were bigger and wider, now twice the size of his hand. Its black claws were longer. Sharper.

A new sound came from the other side of the nearest dog. Bert crept cautiously around on his hands and knees to see what it was. And there along the dog's spine—from the neck to the tail—he saw spikes of gray bone rising out of a dreadful split in the hide. The dog whined, and its tail lashed the ground.

Bert pushed himself to his feet. The dogs were

rousing. The nearest one growled and lifted its head, foam clinging to its jaw. Bert caught a glimpse of terrible, yellow eyes. The dog jerked its head from side to side, and the spittle flew off, spattering Bert's leggings. When he saw the head and how it had transformed, the breath he was about to take snagged in his throat.

"What . . . what are they?" Bert asked the mirror. They weren't dogs anymore, that was certain.

Servants. To do your bidding, the mirror said. *And do you have a task for these beasts?*

Bert grabbed a fist with the other hand and squeezed it. "Of course. Mirror, tell me if the letter to my father has arrived. And tell me where my brother is now."

26

Will walked into the hall of Ambercrest. He felt hot bruises on his arms and legs from the dozens of blows he'd received in his latest session with Andreas. He smiled a little, remembering the handful of times he'd slipped his own sword past the knight's defenses and struck back. A bounce came to his stride despite the aches. But he came to a sudden halt when he saw his father in the corridor before him, waiting with his hands clasped behind his back. Expecting him, obviously.

"Will," his father said simply.

"Yes, Father?" Will said, trying to recall what he might have done wrong.

The baron cocked his head and stared down with one eye narrowed. "It *is* Will, isn't it?"

"Of course, Father!" Will said, wincing.

The baron chuckled. "Oh, it's all right son, I was just joking."

Will's mouth hung open. *Joking?* Now it was his turn to wonder who he was talking to. He took a closer look at his father. The baron shifted his weight from foot to foot, and his glance wandered from the floor to the ceiling. Will wondered what was going on. He didn't know what to do with his hands, so he clasped them behind his own back, just as his father had. He waited with his bottom lip held between his teeth.

The baron finally cleared his throat. And when he spoke it wasn't the usual blustery roar. It was soft, almost a whisper. "I . . . I watched your lessons. With Andreas. You're doing well."

"Thank you, Father. Andreas is . . . He's a good teacher." As usual with his father, Will felt like he had to choose his words carefully.

"Yes, quite good," the baron said. "I've watched for a few days now. From the balcony, usually. I stay in the shadows. . . . I don't want to make you nervous. It's a funny thing. How a stranger can sometimes teach a boy better than his own father." The baron's voice trailed off, and he looked past Will's shoulder, staring at nothing.

"You're a good teacher too," Will said. He didn't really mean it. Anytime his father had tried to teach Bert and him anything, it ended with them crying and Father shouting and storming off. In fact, the baron had given up trying to teach them anything a few years ago.

"No, I'm atrocious. No patience at all," the baron mumbled. There was a pause that seemed eternal. Will wished he could turn and run. Finally his father spoke again. "You like this Andreas, don't you?"

Will's mouth opened seconds before a reply finally emerged like a wary mouse. "He's all right."

"Oh, you can be honest. I know you two have hit it off. And you should hear the way he talks about you." The baron smiled, but it was a sad grin. His shoulders slumped, and he looked ten years older. Will felt a warm itch in the corner of his eye, and when he touched it his finger came away damp. What on Earth was his father trying to tell him?

"The courier arrived with a pair of letters today," the baron said.

Will's eyes widened. "Parley?"

The baron closed his eyes briefly and shook his head. "One of my brother's men. No sign of Parley yet, Will. He was another one of your favorites, wasn't he?"

Will shrank back, wondering if he should feel stung by the words. A look of frustration flashed on the baron's face as if he'd regretted saying them. He reached out to pat Will's shoulder. "Don't lose hope, Son. Parley's a rascal, you know. He'll turn up with an amusing story to explain his delay." Will didn't mean for it to happen, but his shoulder twitched under his father's touch. The baron drew back his hand.

"But about the letters," the baron said. "One was from your uncle Hugh, telling me what a fine young man your brother has been. Obedient and respectful. It was such a happy letter, it's hard to believe your uncle wrote it." Will smiled wanly at the joke.

"The other letter," the baron said, "was from your brother." Will drew in a sharp breath and held it. *Finally!*

He'd waited so long for his brother to write back—the silence was baffling. But why had he written to Father and not him?

"It was a fine letter, written with great care and humility. Your brother asked your mother and me to forgive the two of you for the trouble you caused. And he wondered if we would allow you to visit him at The Crags for a while this summer."

Will blinked up at his father. "Visit?" His voice came out tight and high.

"Yes. Andreas tells me that you and he have been venturing out. He says your fear is weakening. But you have not conquered it entirely."

Will felt a shiver coming over him and fought to control it. "Not entirely, Father. But mostly, I believe."

"Hm," the baron said. "Let me tell you something else. Your mother and I have been talking things over. Many things. We think the lesson has been learned. There's no need for you and Bert to be parted any longer. I decided to send the carriage to bring him back."

Will felt a wave of joy surge through his body. "Really?"

The baron nodded. "Really. But why not have it both ways? Go with the party that's fetching your brother. That way you can accept the invitation and see him all the sooner. And you can travel back together."

Will seized his father around the waist and hugged him. "Thank you, Father!" He felt strong hands pat him on the back and heard his father sniff.

"Of course, it all depends on you being able to make the journey to The Crags. It's a long way. Can you do it?"

Will had his face turned sideways against his father's chest. He hesitated to say the next thing, but he had to. It was the only way he could go. "Do you think Andreas could go with me?"

The hands on his back fell still. "Of course," his father said finally. "I wish I could go myself. But there's an envoy coming from the king. And other business that keeps me here. Certainly, Andreas can go with you, if you think it will help."

"I wish you could come, too," Will said. And he realized he might even have meant it.

His father's hands moved to Will's shoulders and pushed him back to arm's length. "That's the trouble with being a baron, Son. Sometimes all the responsibility gets in the way of the things you'd really like to do. And it distracts you from the things that you ought to be paying more attention to. But when the two of you get back, Will, it will be different here. In a good way, I mean. Your mother and I think we could handle some things better."

"Bert and I can be better, too," Will said. "We won't cause so much trouble."

"Let's call it a bargain, then," the baron said. "We'll do better all around."

27

Harth came into Parley's alcove. As soon as the molton saw the bucket that he carried, it opened its mouth wide like a baby bird. Harth used the black tongs to drop glowing coals down its throat. Then the Dwergh turned to Parley. Parley frowned; the friendly twinkle seemed to be gone from Harth's eye.

"What's the matter, friend?" Parley said. He grunted as he rose to his feet.

"Our task is over," said Harth. "We did not find what we were looking for."

Parley gulped. "I hope this setback hasn't put anybody in a bad mood," he said with a forced chuckle.

Harth's head sagged, and his beard rustled against his chest. "Of course it has. But I've come to tell you that the matter of your fate has been settled."

Parley's brains turned to slush, and his bad leg wobbled. "Hold on—you promised I could have my say before you decided!"

From the corner of his one eye Parley saw dark, stocky shapes fill the entrance to the alcove. The Dwergh were there, all of them. Kholl stepped out from the group.

"Harth says you talk so much there can't be anything left to say," Kholl said.

Parley opened his mouth, but only a feeble chirp came out. Kholl held up one hand.

"Do not fear. You will be spared," the old Dwergh said to Parley's infinite relief. "And freed. But only because Harth has vouched for you. And taken the oath in your name." The Dwergh leader slipped his arms behind his beard and folded them across his chest. Behind him, the others stared—some at the courier, some at Harth. "Do you understand what this means, Par Lee?"

Parley passed a hand over the top of his head and grinned crookedly. "The 'spare Parley' bit is clear enough—and believe me, I'm plenty grateful for that. But the vouch and the oath . . . ?"

"It means that Harth bears responsibility for anything you do that brings us harm. If you speak of what you've seen here and reveal our presence, it will be as if Harth himself has betrayed us. Your transgressions become his. And the punishments that go with it."

Parley's eyebrows threatened to retreat right over the top of his head. "So, for example, if I tell my baron that you're here, and he sends men after you . . ."

"Harth will die," Kholl said calmly.

Parley's head swiveled toward Harth, who stood with his chest thrust forward.

"Harth, I don't know what to say. You did this for me? Your sworn enemy?"

"I never swore such a thing," Harth said. He put a hand into the pocket of his leather shirt, produced a key, and tossed it on the ground where Mokh squatted. "Mokh, *gup-chik*," Harth said to the molton.

The molton picked up the key in its three-fingered hand and slid it into the keyhole on the shackle. The lock popped open, and Parley shook the chain off his ankle. He bent at the waist and held an open hand toward Mokh. "You've treated me well enough, little fellow. Can I shake your hand?" Mokh stared at the palm for a moment, then shrugged and strutted away to stand by Harth's side.

Parley shook his head and chuckled. He lifted his courier's pack and slung it over his shoulder. "Never fear, Harth. You can trust me."

Harth smiled from the depths of his beard. "That is why I took the oath, Par Lee. But before you leave, we want to show you something. So you know that we were not here to take gems or gold from under your nose, but for a greater purpose—one that you must never reveal."

"By all means," Parley said. "I enjoy our little strolls. And it will give me time to come up with a reason why I've been missing all these days."

The journey started the same as when they'd led Parley to the chamber of the seven coffins. But this time they turned into the left-hand passage instead of the right.

Before, even the ancient Kholl had walked with

purpose and vigor. Now all the Dwergh's heads sagged as they proceeded, and Parley knew their disappointment was bitter. He wanted to tell Harth and Kholl that he was sorry, that he wished their efforts had not been unrewarded. But neither of them was talking. And he didn't want to risk offending them. Who knew? They might change their minds about letting him go.

The corridor ended in a strange sight: a square door made of glossy, black stone, tall enough to suit a Dwergh. Parley could see the lantern's light reflected in its surface. The door was engraved with strange writing that ran along the top, sides, and bottom, like a frame.

Oddly, the door was undamaged—not a scratch that Parley could see—while a narrow tunnel had been clawed into the solid rock a few strides to the right. There was a pile of shattered stone and dust by the entrance.

"I presume nobody had the key?" Parley said, breaking the silence at last.

Kholl peered up sternly at the courier. "No key can open that door. Nor can any hammer knock it down. The magic that protects it is too great."

"Magic, you say?" said Parley.

Kholl nodded. There was a heavy pick leaning against the wall. He lifted it and swung it at the door in a wide, sweeping arc. It struck the black stone and bounced back with nearly as much force as Kholl had delivered. Kholl let the pick drop to the ground and rubbed his hands together. "Look," the old Dwergh said, pointing at the spot where the pick had struck.

Parley brought his one eye close to the door. "I see that you've made a little . . ." he started to say, and then the words faded. There *was* a tiny gash in the door—just a nick, really. But as he watched, the wound healed as if black oil welled up from the inside and hardened in an instant.

"That is why we had to tunnel in through the side," Harth said. "But even the rock itself seemed enchanted, and resisted our efforts for many months. We only pierced through into his lair a few hours ago."

"*His* lair? *Whose* lair?" Parley asked, stepping back from the door.

"Never fear, Par Lee," Kholl said. "He is long dead. Only his possessions lay inside."

Parley looked at Harth, questioning.

"Come inside with us, Par Lee," Harth said, and he crawled into the tunnel, holding the lamp before him with one hand.

Parley looked uneasily at the narrow passageway. The unpleasant thought occurred to him that this might be a ruse—that he'd been sentenced to die after all, and was being lured to his execution. He felt a hand on his shoulder.

"Go on, Par Lee," Kholl said. "I will follow."

Parley gulped and nodded. He crawled into the hole. The light of Harth's lantern was ahead, like a rising moon at the end of the rough, black tunnel. It was wide enough for a Dwergh's brawny shoulders, but so low that Parley couldn't get up on his knees—he had to put his belly to the ground and inch along like a caterpillar. *Would have been easier if you'd taken your pack off*, he chided himself. Some dust went up his nose, and a sneezing fit slowed him halfway through. But he finally emerged at the other end, holding his breath as he stuck his head out. Harth was there, offering a hand to help him up. Parley stepped away from the opening, so Kholl could follow. As the eldest Dwergh squeezed out of the hole like a great shaggy mouse, the courier looked around.

It wasn't a large room, maybe ten steps across. At first Parley thought it was round. But a second glance showed him it was a series of flat, smoothly polished walls coming together. He counted them. *Seven. Of course.*

He saw the inner face of the impervious door, as glossy and black as the outer side, untouched even by dust. And around the chamber, he saw things both commonplace and strange. There was a chest with its lid open, and it was filled with chalices—gold, silver, copper, and some metal that was pure white. There were pieces of armor on the ground. There was an anvil, and a hammer with a head as big as Parley's. There was a globe of smoke-colored glass on a pedestal, and sealed urns and jars. And on a tall, round table in the center of the room—chest-high for the Dwergh, waist-high for Parley—there was an assortment of smaller items.

Daggers. Medallions. Seven-sided disks of metal, like coins. Parley's eye went to a pair of strange candlesticks that looked like intertwined snakes with their open mouths pointed skyward. The candles had been in them so long that the wax melted without the benefit of flame, and they lay on the table like wilted flowers.

"His name was Khorgon," Harth said. "The most powerful Dwergh sorcerer who ever lived. He died hundreds of years ago. But before his death he collected many magical objects—some dangerous, some not, some he discovered, some he devised. He hid them away in secret places scattered across your land and ours. Mokh is one of those objects. We found the molton in another chamber like this, under a hill many miles from here. But we have always sought one object in particular. A most dangerous thing. We prayed we would find it here, but that was not the will of the earth."

Parley couldn't contain his curiosity. "What was that thing that was so dangerous? If you don't mind me asking?"

"A mirror," Parley finally moaned, after a long drink of water restored his voice. "That's what you just said, isn't it?"

"What do you know about this?" Harth said. Kholl stared at the courier with a fierce glint in his dark eyes.

"Oh me. Oh dear," Parley said. He slumped on the floor of the sorcerer's chamber. He shrugged off his pack, stuck a hand inside, and then paused to look sheepishly up at the Dwergh. "I've done something less than honorable. I'm ashamed to tell you, really. But you have to understand how bored I was, locked up like that. You know, if Mokh had just played dice with me, I never would have—"

"Tell us what you know!" snapped Kholl, strangling the air before him.

"Right! Well . . ." Parley began. He pulled the roll of parchment from his pack. "I sort of opened this letter. It's from the baron's son Bert to his brother, Will. Bert is staying at The Crags for the summer."

"The Crags," whispered Harth. Kholl leaned forward. His black eyes looked as if they might burst into flame.

"That's right, The Crags," Parley said. He coughed and tasted dust. He wanted another sip of water, but thought Kholl might throttle him if he delayed another second. "Well, you see, according to the letter, Bert . . . *found* something. In a . . . you know, hidden chamber. Under The Crags."

"He found a mirror," Kholl said.

"Yes," Parley said. Kholl was so quiet for so long that Parley risked another sip. He stuck the little cork back into the skin and wiped his mouth. "Listen, boys, you said this thing was dangerous. Bert's not in trouble, is he? He's very dear to me, that lad."

Kholl and Harth exchanged a glance and a frown.

"Tell me! Is Bert in danger?" Parley asked. His lip trembled, and his one eye blinked madly.

"Read the letter to us, Par Lee," Harth said.

Parley sighed. He peeled the wax away from the parchment. "I'm so ashamed. This is the second time I've broken the seal. After I repaired it so nicely, too. No one would have noticed. Well, here's what it says: 'Dear Will, by the time you finish reading this, you'll wish it was you that came to The Crags after all. I just made the most amazing discovery. . . .'"

Kholl listened with his fingertips pressed together over his nose. Harth tugged his beard and paced around the seven-sided chamber.

When Parley reached the part about the candlestick that unlocked the hidden door, his eye went to the similar object on the sorcerer's table. He read on about the secret stairs. The hidden chamber. The throne. And the mirror. He cringed, and his face turned as warm and red as the setting sun when he got to the last words: "'Remember that everything I have written is a secret. Hide this letter, or better yet burn it, and tell no one.'" The courier coughed and lowered the parchment. "Well, shame on me for prying."

There was a long silence. Harth stared at Kholl while the elder Dwergh brooded with his eyes closed. Harth finally spoke. "Can there be any doubt, any at all?"

"Hidden under the castle of The Crags. You told us once it might be there, Harth," Kholl said. "We should have listened."

"But you were right, Kholl. It was too risky to approach, under that man's suspicious gaze."

"Listen," Parley said in a voice that quavered, "what's this all about? You haven't answered my question. Is Bert in danger?"

"He is," Kholl said wearily. "As is everyone he knows. Including us, for that matter. Par Lee, you must hear the story of the Mirror of Khorgon as we return to the others. And then we will decide what is to be done."

Before they left, Harth sorted through the items that remained in the sorcerer's chamber. He filled two large sacks and one small one with objects. He and Kholl carried the large bags and Mokh took the smaller one.

Parley protested that he could carry his share, but Harth would not hear of it. They pushed the sacks ahead of them through the tunnel and bustled back the way they'd come. Parley marveled at the energy of the elder Dwergh. *One hundred and sixty-seven years old, and I can barely keep pace*, he thought as he puffed along between the two of them and their stone servant.

"Walk beside me, Par Lee. I will make this as brief as I can," Kholl said. "The deeds of Khorgon were great. You see, every now and then, we Dwergh encounter strange and terrible things as we explore the cracks and crevices under the hide of the earth. Serpents. Trolls. Spirits. Goblins. Khorgon vanquished scores of these, with axe and incantation. And the more he slew, the greater his pride became, until he deemed himself invincible. He foolishly chose to confront the most evil thing we Dwergh ever encountered. It was called the 'Ulgonog,' the Unspeakable. It was a demon, of sorts, that lived deep in a watery cave—so hideous to behold, it could drive you mad to look at it. The Ulgonog had a fearsome power: It could see from afar. It knew what its enemies planned and when someone approached. And when you drew near, the Ulgonog whispered promises, offering to make your fondest wishes come true. Once you heard its voice, you could not resist. You walked— no, you ran—into its lair. And when you crawled out days later, your heart and mind were gone. You were a babbling, drooling animal, as hollow as an egg drained of its yolk. That is the way of the Ulgonog: It feasts on souls."

Parley's head sank between his shoulders. "I never dreamed of such a horror. So what did Khorgon do?"

"He decided to capture the Ulgonog instead of destroying it. Why? So he could boast of it, I suppose. Or perhaps he thought he could make it serve him and become all the greater for it. Khorgon's apprentice, a wise and trusted Dwergh, tried to dissuade him, but the proud sorcerer would not listen. His plan was to weaken the Ulgonog, and then trap it. And he had a powerful weapon to help him: an amulet that shielded his mind from the demon's prying eye. With this amulet around his neck, Khorgon crept into the lair of the Ulgonog and attacked with all the spell-craft he could muster. They say the ground shook and rumbled, and smoke and fire billowed out of the earth, and lightning seared the heavens, and everything stank of sulfur and charred flesh. Khorgon himself was nearly exhausted. But, finally, when he thought the time was right, and the Ulgonog was about to lose its earthly form and dissolve into nothing, the sorcerer brought forth his trap."

"But . . . what sort of trap . . . could catch a demon?" Parley asked, out of breath.

"Not the sort you'd expect. This was a cage made of gold and glass. It had the form of a mirror."

Parley stumbled at the word, so that Kholl had to

reach over and steady him. "A mirror?" Parley sputtered. "Not the same . . . !" He looked over his shoulder at Harth, who nodded gravely as he followed.

"Yes. But in the end, it was the sorcerer who was trapped. Because the Ulgonog sensed that it was beaten, that it was about to fade from existence without the protection of the physical form that the sorcerer had ruined. So it did what Khorgon wanted: It let the mirror draw it in. The mirror that was meant to be its dungeon became its refuge instead. A place to rest and heal. But like a sly snake, the demon slithered around and probed its prison, seeking a way out. Eventually it discovered a flaw in the powerful spell that contained it. The Ulgonog whispered to Khorgon like it whispered to a thousand victims before. The mighty sorcerer foolishly set his protective amulet aside, and he was quickly seduced. Then Khorgon turned to evil. He used his magic to murder and enslave, bewitch his friends, transform animals into horrific monsters to terrorize his foes—"

"Wait, please . . . I need rest," Parley panted. He stopped and leaned against a pillar of rock. "And water." He took a long sip from the skin. "Tell me, how can you know all this? What, did Khorgon tell it?"

"Khorgon's apprentice," Kholl said. "He witnessed everything, and barely escaped after Khorgon was possessed. But perhaps Harth should tell you that part."

Parley turned to Harth. The younger Dwergh was

gulping water, and he wiped his mouth and brushed drops off his beard.

"That apprentice was my father's father," Harth said. "He took the amulet with him when he fl ed, so Khorgon could not find him."

Parley rolled his eyes toward the dark rock above. "Honestly, this is more than my simple mind can handle."

"You've heard most of what you need to know," Harth said, picking up the story while Kholl drank. "Once the Ulgonog—the mirror—possessed Khorgon, an age of terror began. And it lasted until Khorgon was used up, completely mad. Then Khorgon disappeared, taking the mirror with him. Somehow the mirror passed itself to a new owner. And once that victim was drained of life, the Ulgonog did it again—often sleeping for years in some secret place where its previous owner hid it away and probably perished at its side. But every time the mirror surfaced, dreadful things happened. New victims were possessed. Their evil deeds are legend to the Dwergh: Pankho the Cruel. Tilos the Beheader. The Robber King."

"And the Witch-Queen," Parley whispered. "It was this . . . *mirror* that drove her mad."

Kholl grunted. "Yes, the Witch-Queen. Forgive us, Par Lee. We should have suspected what was happening. But the Ulgonog was always the scourge of Dwergh, and never your folk. If we were wiser, we could have ended this a hundred years ago." The old Dwergh dug his calloused hand into his beard and rubbed his jaw, brooding. Then his gaze turned back to Parley. "What sort of boy is this baron's son, the one at The Crags?"

"Bert?" Parley said, stiffening. "He's a good lad. With a good heart. He's mischievous, but what boy isn't? And just a little . . ." Parley clamped his teeth on his bottom lip, biting off the word.

"A little what, Par Lee?" Kholl said, firm but quiet.

"I don't know," Parley said. "Ambitious? Eager to . . . rule?" He looked wide-eyed at the Dwergh. "But he's just a child. What use would a child be to such a . . . *monster?*"

Harth picked up his sack and slung it over his shoulder again. "Come. We need to hurry."

29

Two of the baron's men rode ahead of Will and two behind him. Between them the carriage rumbled along with nobody on board except Matthias on the driver's perch. Will and Andreas were on their horses beside it.

"How are you feeling?" Andreas said, leaning over and keeping his voice low.

"Not bad," Will replied. He took a deep breath and held it before exhaling. His jaw ached, and he knew it came from clenching it tight for hours. *Maybe this wasn't such a great idea*, he thought. The ache in his jaw became an urge to yawn, and he opened his mouth wide. The yawn seemed to last a minute. Sleep was elusive the night before, while the party rested under the stars. Every time he dozed off he woke a short while later, gasping for air, pawing at an invisible weight that pressed down on his chest.

The way narrowed as it climbed and became the Cliff Road. Will and Andreas had to spur their horses to the front of the carriage, because there was little room on either side. To the left, the thick forest swallowed the rising land. And to the right, the valley fell away as the cliff grew, sheer and tall.

This was the coolest day in a while, and the gloomiest. Thick clouds hung low overhead. Will looked up, wondering if it might rain, hoping it wouldn't. Andreas would make him ride in the carriage, but Will felt better, braver, on his own horse.

He heard something snap in the trees beside them. He turned to peer into the thick woods. A moment later, a shadowy form rushed across a narrow space between some trees. Will craned his neck toward the spot, staring. And just when he thought he'd only imagined it, he glimpsed a second shape. This time he saw it long enough to judge its speed—the same as theirs. *Tracking us*, he thought. He looked at Andreas, and saw the knight staring at the same spot through narrowed lids.

"Did you see . . . ?" Will said.

"Yes," Andreas replied.

"What was it?"

"Wolves, I think. Just looking us over, I'm sure. They'd never attack a party like this."

That should have made Will feel better, but his nerves still jangled. That glimpse had hinted at the creature's size. It looked awfully big, even for a wolf. And the shape—he'd never seen anything like it. It was vaguely canine, but with shoulders as thick as a bear's and . . . *spikes* on its back? Had he really seen that or was his nervous mind playing tricks? He shivered and scanned the forest, both eager and afraid to see more.

A twig cracked in the trees. There was a rustle, and Will saw a branch shake as something struck it. He heard a metallic whisper nearby. Andreas had drawn his sword. Will wondered if he should draw his as well, but his hands clutched his reins so tight he wasn't sure he could let go.

Behind them, past the carriage, one of the soldiers shrieked. "What's that? What's that thing? There's something in the trees!"

"More than one!" another cried.

"Did you see its eyes? Did you see those teeth?" the first said, his voice quaking.

Andreas edged his horse between Will and the woods. His eyes darted ahead and behind, and he looked with regret at the precipice to their right. The cliff was so high now that the tallest trees in the valley barely reached the level of the road. "What would the general of the east say about this situation, Will?" he called out of the side of his mouth.

Will couldn't talk until he'd gulped. "He'd say we chose bad terrain. And we should've—" but he didn't get the rest out, because he spotted a nightmarish face in the woods, between a pair of trees. It wasn't running this time. It just stared. At *him*.

It was no wolf. And it wasn't a bear or a badger or anything else he'd ever seen before, alive or dead. Its eyes were glazed white, and its nose was a gnarled black lump. Its mouth was horribly wide. Dreadful yellow teeth as long as fingers jutted from the jaws at strange angles in such disarray that the thing could never entirely close its mouth. And as if all those fangs weren't enough, more teeth had punched through the skin of its throat and snout. Strings of rubbery drool dangled from the gaping maw.

There was only one thing Will could imagine it might be. A name sprang suddenly to mind, the only one that made sense: the Beast of The Crags.

The beast lurched down and out of sight. Will saw branches shake farther ahead—the beast had darted ahead of the party.

"Get in the carriage," Andreas said calmly. He raised his sword. "Driver, men—everyone stop!"

Matthias, who'd gone as gray as the clouds overhead, pulled back on his reins and stopped the carriage. Will swung his leg over his horse and dropped to the ground. He heard a shout from ahead and behind, almost at the same time. Beyond the riders in front, a fearsome creature had leaped out of the woods. It crouched low to the road, whipped its head from side to side, and snapped at the air. Now that Will saw the entire thing in daylight, out of the murky trees, his mind didn't want to believe what it was seeing. The beast had a leathery hide with ragged tufts of hair. Along its spine and its sides, knobs and plates and spikes of bone had erupted crazily from the flesh, forming a skeletal armor. Its tail ended in a heart-shaped lump of bone that looked as if it could crack a man's skull as it lashed back and forth.

The horses panicked, dancing madly backward while the men fought to control them. Behind the carriage, Will heard whinnies and shouts, and he knew that a second beast was on the road. *A trap*, his mind shouted. *They planned this!*

"Get inside, Will!" Andreas shouted, and Will remembered what he was supposed to do. But as he turned toward the carriage he saw something explode from the trees and rush directly at him. *Another one! How many now?* His brain screamed at him to run, but his feet felt as if they were nailed to the road.

"*Move!*" Andreas commanded in a voice so loud that it must have torn the flesh inside the knight's throat. Will broke for the carriage. It was only a few steps. But he knew he'd hesitated too long, and the thing would reach him first.

The beast crouched and sprang. Andreas swung his sword, but his horse reared in fright, and the blade sliced the air above the creature's head. All Will could do was let his legs collapse underneath him, fall to the ground, and hope the beast would pass over him. He threw his arms across his head and felt something hard and sharp tear his sleeve, and heard the *clack, clack* of teeth gnashing. The beast had leaped too high. The claws of its rear legs scraped across Will's shoulder as it sailed over him and sent Will tumbling along the ground, farther from the safety of the carriage.

Will uncovered his head, uncertain even of which direction he was facing. He turned left and right, and realized what happened: The beast had leaped across the road entirely. Its hind legs were over the edge of the cliff, and it scrambled to get back onto the road. Andreas had dismounted, and he charged at the creature with his shield in one hand and his sword poised over his other shoulder. Will heard growls and snaps everywhere and the terrible whinny of a horse in agony.

"Come on, Will!" shouted Matthias. The carriage rocked back and forth as its pair of horses lunged and reared, and Matthias struggled with the reins. Will ran for the door, wrenched it open, and pulled it shut. But it bounced open again. He looked down and saw the end of the sheathed sword that he wore sticking out at the bottom of the door, blocking it. He twisted his body, pulled the sword in, and slammed the door. Then he looked through the window to see what had happened to Andreas.

The beast heaved itself up just as Andreas brought his sword down. There was a clang as the blade struck a knob of bone on the top of the thing's head. The beast snapped at the knight, gnashing its jumble of teeth, and gathered itself to spring at him. Andreas brought his shield up as the beast leaped, and there was a thunderous crash of skull against metal. The knight fell on his back and the beast landed nearby on its side. The creature was up again a second later before Andreas could recover. The knight would have died there if not for a frantic horse with no rider that dashed by, its eyes huge and its teeth bared. The beast snapped at it, and the horse reared up on two legs, pawing at the air with its hooves. The horse stumbled backward, too close to the cliff. One hoof slipped over the ledge, and the rest of the poor animal followed.

Andreas was on his feet again, thrusting his shield at the beast. "Go!" he shouted to Matthias, and "Clear a path!" to the men ahead.

Matthias was eager to obey. He seized his whip and cracked the air over his horse's tails. The carriage leaped forward. Will leaned out the window to see if Andreas was all right. A breath stuck in his throat as he watched the beast ignore the knight and race after the carriage, digging clumps of dirt with its wicked claws as it ran.

Will's hand came up and clutched his neck. "It wants *me*."

The carriage rumbled past two of the baron's men, who'd forced another one of the creatures to the side of the road, so the driver could pass. That beast leaped up the slope and into the trees. It emerged again beyond the men and joined the other in pursuit of the carriage. They barked as they ran. To Will's horror the bark sounded like a word: "*Death! Death!*"

There was a loud crash of wood splintering and nails popping. The carriage rocked high to one side and nearly tipped. Will heard a shout and saw Matthias tumble past the window. He had a moment to consider his plight: alone in a carriage with no driver, pulled by terrified horses, careening along a narrow road at the top of a cliff. And then, as a blast of hot stinking breath washed over him, he realized he wasn't alone at all.

CHAPTER

30

Will turned to see the face of the beast inches from his own. It barked at him, loud as thunder. And there was no mistaking it: *"Death!"*

The head stretched toward him, mouth open wide. Will leaned back to avoid being caught between the rows of jagged teeth that gnashed together.

The beast had smashed a hole in the door on the left of the carriage. Its head and one of its legs were through, and it was trying to wriggle in the rest of the way. The hole splintered at the edges and widened as the creature thrashed back and forth. A second paw muscled through. Every one of the black claws was like a blunt dagger. The beast drew itself in another foot, and it lunged at Will again, forcing him to scramble to the other side of the carriage. He felt a tooth scrape his knee.

Will tried to draw his sword, but the space was too cramped. He reached to his other side, where a knife was slung, and unsheathed it. The carriage lurched again, and he heard a heavy thud and a snarl from above. *Another one on the roof!* But still the carriage rolled faster as the crazed horses ran. The beat of their hooves sounded like a hailstorm.

The wood crunched as the first beast squeezed its broad shoulders through the hole. Will pressed his back against the other door. The beast strained forward, stretching its neck, and Will turned his face to the side as the jaws snapped shut again. Flecks of hot drool spattered his cheek. It suddenly felt as if his heart had stopped midbeat. He couldn't move his arms, and his legs were shaking. He was dimly aware that a high-pitched moan was slipping out from his mouth and that he was crying.

Then words came to him: *What's on the other side of my fear?*

He still had the knife. With both hands on the grip, he screamed and shoved it as hard as he could into the underside of the monster's jaw.

The beast roared. Will glimpsed the blade inside its gaping mouth. The creature thrashed wildly and slipped out through the hole it had made. The carriage bounced high, and Will heard a gruesome crunch, and he knew the rear wheel must have run over the fallen beast.

Something hard and sharp slammed into Will's back. He fell to the floor of the carriage, grimacing from the stinging pain. He looked back to see a clawed paw reaching through the other door, swiping at the space he'd just left.

And then something went wrong with the carriage.

It wobbled crazily as if a wheel was loose. There was a snapping, wrenching noise, and the sound of hammering hooves changed direction and grew more distant. *The horses have broken away from the carriage,* Will realized, as he lay on his back. *But it's still rolling!*

The carriage veered left, bounced off something unyielding—a tree or a boulder—and swerved right. And then, a strange quiet came. The only thing Will heard was the *squeak, squeak* of wheels spinning madly. His body floated as if he were light as air.

I'm over the cliff, he thought. And in the moment that followed, he had time to wish that he'd seen his brother again before the end.

The carriage came to a violent stop, sooner than he thought possible. He was hurled sideways into the cushioned seat. The carriage rolled until its front pointed up, and Will tumbled down to the back. He glanced at the door. The monstrous paw was gone. His breath came in great, heaving gasps as he lay there and waited for the next horrible development that would surely come.

But for a long while nothing happened. The carriage rocked gently as if there was a baby inside that needed sleep. Will bent his elbows and wrists, his knees and ankles. Nothing seemed broken, though he couldn't begin to count the bruises. His instincts told him that all was not yet well, so he stood slowly until he could look through the hole that the beast had torn in the side of the carriage.

All he could see was the gray face of the cliff. He cautiously edged his head out of the hole, though he doubted the beast was still with him. When he saw what was below, he gasped.

The carriage was suspended high over the ground, forty feet or more, as if frozen in midfall. *But how?* He looked out the other side of the carriage, and saw the broad trunk of a tree, almost within reach. He poked his hand through the window and quickly drew it in, still worried that a paw might slash down. But it didn't. He eased his head back out and saw that a thick branch had pierced the spokes of the front wheel of the carriage. That was the only thing holding it up. It would be a lethal fall if the carriage broke loose. He took a closer look at the ground and saw the crumpled, still body of a beast.

Will heard an ominous creak, and the carriage started to tilt. The branch sagged under its weight, and he saw the limb begin to crack, exposing the tender white wood under its gray bark. He didn't wait to see how long the carriage might stay aloft. He pushed the door open— the carriage was sideways, so it flopped straight down— and searched desperately for another branch to cling to. There was a snapping sound, and the carriage fell free. Will leaped away as it plummeted. He threw himself at a thick cluster of leaves.

He gripped the branches with all the strength he could muster. They were thin and supple, and they bent from his weight, easing his fall. Below, he heard the carriage shatter on the ground. He looked beneath his dangling feet and saw one of the wheels bounce away from the wreckage, past the fallen beast.

The branches he clung to bent as far as they would go, but he was still dangerously far from the ground. He'd come to a stop near a slender birch tree. Will wrapped his legs around the birch and seized it with both arms, letting the branches that saved him spring back toward the sky. He stayed there a moment to catch his breath and gather his wits while the supple tree swayed back and forth under his weight. Then he relaxed his hug on the trunk and slid toward the ground. The bark rubbed his skin raw through his sleeves and pants, but it was a safe way to descend. Before long he felt his feet touch the earth. He dropped to his knees and covered his face with his hands, unsure which would overcome him first: laughter or tears.

It occurred to him that he might still be in a fix. He looked at the cliff above and saw a pair of the beasts, nosing around the edge, looking for a way down. One of them turned its head to face him. Its ugly mouth opened, and Will heard the unnatural bark again: "Death! Death!"

"What do you want from me?" he screamed. "Leave me alone!" He picked up a stone and flung it at the beasts, but it clattered off the sheer wall, woefully short of its target. The creatures turned as one, and they ran back down the road the way that Will's party had come, toward the lower terrain where they could enter the valley, double back, and track him down.

Will wondered where he should go next. He couldn't see Andreas and the others. He wondered how far the carriage had rolled before it went off the cliff.

He put his hands on either side of his mouth and shouted, "Andreas! Can you hear me? Matthias? Can anybody hear me?" There was no answer. *Maybe I should stay here*, he thought. *They'll come and look for me eventually. If any of them are still alive.* The thought sent a shiver through him. *No, they can't be dead. Andreas can fight, he'll make it.* He pondered the wisdom of staying put. It would be a footrace between the men and the beasts.

He made up his mind to put his faith in Andreas and wait by the wreck of the carriage. It seemed like the smartest thing to do. But then his heart jolted as he heard a deep, rumbling growl behind him. He whirled, expecting to see another one of those monsters standing there. But it was the fallen beast, lying on its side next to the wreck.

How can you not be dead? Will wondered. The beast's eyes were still closed. One of its clawed feet twitched, and the ugly, knobbed head wobbled off the ground.

Will froze, trying to avoid its attention. He hoped the thing would fall unconscious again. The beast shook its head, sneezed, and spat out a bloody fang the size of a dinner knife. It pawed at the ground with one foot and tried to sit up. Will's hand moved to his side and touched an empty sheath where his sword should have been. *Lost it when I was rolling around in the carriage,* he figured. He thought of trying to retrieve it from the wreck, but that would take him closer to the monster.

The beast opened its eyes and saw Will. Thick, bubbly drool spilled out between its teeth. It hacked and snorted and redoubled its effort to stand.

Will decided that staying put might not be the best decision after all. He needed a new plan, and fast. He looked to the lower end of the valley. *If I go that way, who will I meet first?* He had the awful feeling that it might be more of the beasts. He glanced at the cliff, but dismissed the idea of climbing it; too steep, too dangerous. And he'd had enough of falling, thank you.

He heard a scraping sound and saw the beast crawl toward him. One of its back legs was broken.

What do I do? he wondered, backing away from the creeping monster. He remembered something from those decaying translations at Ambercrest: *Exploit any advantage over the enemy.* There was one he knew of: People could understand signs, and animals could not. He dug his heel into the soft earth and carved a straight line, then capped it with an inverted *V*. It made an arrow that pointed in the direction he'd decided to go.

Toward The Crags.

It was closer than Ambercrest. His uncle's castle was

only a few hours away, he figured. All he had to do was follow the road.

He started to run. Before he left the wreck of the carriage behind for good, he turned to see if the beast was still dragging itself after him. The creature had paused in its pursuit. It clawed at the earth where he'd dug his arrow. Erasing the message. Will's mouth fell open, and his hand came up and covered it. *This is crazy.*

When the beast was done, it came after him again. Not crawling this time—it hobbled on three legs. It was healing.

With a whimper Will turned and ran again. *To The Crags.* Bert was there, waiting for him. He'd be safe at The Crags if he could only make it there.

CHAPTER

31

Will stopped to rest his aching legs and wipe the sweat off his forehead. From the way the cliff was descending, he thought he might be able to climb onto the road soon. He turned to see if the beast was catching up. The blasted thing was relentless. Thankfully it still wasn't moving too fast, and Will was far enough ahead that he could no longer see it through the sparse trees and tall grass of the valley.

But it still barked at him. "*Death! Death!*" And then, much farther away, Will heard an answering cry from more of the creatures: "*Death! Death! Death!*"

Leave me alone, Will thought grimly. He ran through the tall grass, wondering how much farther he could go before he was worn out. Then he heard a familiar sound ahead: the whinny of a horse. He found a surge of energy and sprinted, calling out, "Hello! Is someone there? Hello!"

"Who's that?" a stranger replied. Will ran toward the voice and saw a thin, young man standing near his horse, which was tethered to a tree. The man held a dead hare by the ears. He had a sparse beard, long neck, and prominent Adam's apple. As Will ran toward him, the man scowled and shouted, shaking the hare with his fist.

"Hey—you're not supposed to be here! You could get strung up for poaching, you know. This valley is for Hugh Charmaigne's hunters only. *Lord* Hugh Charmaigne."

Will eyed the horse gratefully. He bent over with his chest heaving and his hands on his knees, and squeezed words out between gulps of air. "I'm . . . Lord Charmaigne's nephew . . . son of the baron . . . how far to . . . The Crags?"

The man's forehead wrinkled. "The baron's son? But what are you doing here?"

"Attacked . . . by beasts . . . like the Beast of The Crags . . ."

"Beast of The Crags? There ain't been one of those for a hundred years, if there was ever one at all! Are you pulling my leg, Master Son-of-the-Baron?"

Will lost all patience. "I *am* the baron's son, and there *was* a beast! If you want to see one, all you have to do is wait!"

The hunter had his mouth open to retort, but then the beast barked again: *"Death! Death!"* And the following barks came, almost as close. The hunter turned his face toward the sound, and stared with his mouth stuck in that open position.

"What's your name, sir?" Will asked.

"Gunther," came the reply, weak and distracted. His Adam's apple bobbed up and down as he swallowed nervously.

Will remembered the tone his father took when he wanted something done right away. He puffed his chest and did his best impersonation. "Gunther, I am Will Charmaigne, son of Baron Charmaigne and nephew of Lord Charmaigne. You must take me to The Crags, on that horse. For your safety as well as mine. Now!"

A hundred yards away, a cluster of bushes shook and the raging beast clawed out into the open, snarling and limping toward them. "I've decided to take your word for it," Gunther said. He was halfway between a daze and a panic as he held the hare out toward Will. "Hold this, will you?"

Will tossed the dead hare over his shoulder. He looked at the beast again—it was putting weight on the broken leg now, getting healthier with every step. Gunther fumbled with the leather strap that tethered his horse to a tree. Finally it came undone. The hunter scrambled into the saddle and extended a hand. Will clasped Gunther's wrist and swung up behind him. A moment later the horse thumped down the valley, carrying the two of them away.

When the beast realized its prey had escaped, it threw its head back and roared.

"Mirror," said Bert, "Tell me: What has become of my brother, who would steal everything I desire?"

Once again, light flashed from the depths of the glass, and a crystal hum filled the room. Ripples spread across the cold surface and disappeared under the edges. The mirror spoke. *Your brother lives. He was not slain by the beasts.*

"What!" Bert screamed, hammering both arms of the throne with his fists. "They should have gotten him! How could he escape?"

He was fortunate, said the mirror. *But now the fortune is yours, because one of your uncle's hunters has found the boy and brings him here. To you.*

"Here? Will is coming *here?*" Bert said. He felt something in his chest as if a dart had struck his heart. And he thought he heard an inner voice, too far and faint to understand. He shook his head to clear it. "I must find Uncle Hugh and tell him what to do. . . . I'll have Will seized as soon as he arrives. Yes, I'll bring him down here, chain him up . . . He'll be sorry he ever wanted what was mine! Mirror, tell me, where is my uncle now?"

Another ripple, another hum. *He walks the walls of The Crags. Waiting for your next instruction.*

Bert raced for the Tunnel of Stars.

33

Parley's feet ached. He couldn't believe they'd walked this far without encountering someone who could speed their journey.

"Are you still there, Harth?" he called into the trees at his side.

"I am," Harth replied.

"You know, if you folk hadn't cooked my horse, we'd be miles away by now."

A low chuckle came from the trees. "We keep no stables in our mines, sadly. And we couldn't risk your horse being found."

"Well, it's a shame, that's all I'm—hold on, someone's coming!" Parley stepped into the middle of the road. This was promising—there were certainly horses heading their way. More than a few, by the sound of it. Parley exhaled on the fat ring on his finger and rubbed it on his shirt to shine it. The ring bore the baron's mark, proof that the courier was on the baron's business. He wasn't sure if it carried enough authority for him to commandeer someone's horse and cart, but he was determined to find out.

The hoof beats came closer. "They're in a hurry,

whoever they are," Parley said toward the trees where Harth stayed hidden. He didn't hear the squeak of wheels that he'd hoped for. His plan—*a shaky plan*, he admitted with a grimace was to keep Harth hidden until he got close to Ambercrest. A wagon or cart where the Dwergh could hide would be best. Harth was an enemy of the kingdom, after all, and things could get sticky if he was spotted. Frankly they'd probably both be killed on the spot. But if he could get Harth near the castle, he could send word to the baron, begging him to meet with a stranger who had information about a threat to his son. And not just information: also a plan to save the boy.

Parley was wondering what he might say to the baron at that moment, when a group of men came into view. His jaw slackened when he realized who the riders were.

"It's some of the baron's soldiers—and a knight!" he called to Harth, shooting the words out of the side of his mouth. *Looks like a knight anyway. I would have preferred a farmer on a cart*, he thought. *This bunch will ask too many questions. And they'll have Harth's head if they see him.* But time was wasting, and he didn't dare pass up the chance for transportation. *I'll talk to them, at least.* He waved his hands over his head.

The men came at a reckless pace with the knight ahead of the other three. The knight slowed his horse, but didn't stop. He was a tall, long-legged fellow with a crooked nose and brown hair down to his shoulders. "Trust me, sir, you don't want to get in my way right now," he said to Parley. And Parley could tell he meant it. Their eyes met as the knight rode past. There was a terrible expression on the man's face—a duet of anguish and anger.

Parley suddenly remembered the ring. He thrust his fist toward the soldiers that followed and called up, "Stop, all of you! This is the baron's mark! I'm on the baron's business, and I insist that you stop!"

The knight turned to glare at Parley. "And I am on the baron's business as well. But my business is graver than yours, I'll wager. Because I must inform the baron that his son is dead."

Parley's bad leg buckled, and he dropped to his knees. The earth tilted beneath him, and the sun dimmed. He clapped his hands over his mouth.

"Parley?" one of the soldiers cried. "Look, boys, it's Parley!"

Parley's good eye was squeezed shut. He heard the *clip-clop* of hooves as the knight's horse turned and trotted, and then the grim fellow's voice. "This is Parley? The courier that's been missing all these weeks?" The knight's boots thumped on the road next to him.

Parley opened his eye and clutched the knight's leg. "What do you mean the baron's son is dead? Which son?"

"We were bringing Will to The Crags," the knight said in a hoarse voice. "We were attacked by . . . a pack of creatures. Things I've never seen before."

"Monsters," one of the soldiers muttered.

"Beasts of The Crags," said another.

Parley rubbed a sleeve across his cheeks. "Oh, Will, I'm so sorry. Too late . . . I came too late," he said, sniffing.

"Parley, my name is Andreas," the knight said, dropping to one knee. He put a hand on the courier's shoulder. "Will always spoke well of you. If you want to blame someone, blame me. When the beasts came, I ordered Will into the carriage. But the carriage went out of control . . . the driver fell and the horses broke away. The carriage went off the cliff a few miles back. We found it smashed to pieces in the valley. And . . . blood inside. But no sign of the boy."

"Oh, Bert, what have you done?" Parley moaned.

"Bert? What are you talking about, Parley?" Andreas squeezed the courier's shoulder.

Parley blinked and focused. He looked Andreas in the eye. "Bert's in . . . danger. We have to save him— we can't lose both of them! You have to get me to Ambercrest."

Andreas had Parley by both shoulders now. "What did you mean? You made it sound like that attack was Bert's doing!"

"No . . . well, yes. Yes and no!" Parley said, somehow shaking his head and nodding at the same time. "Listen to me, Andreas. I have to tell you something. You won't believe me at first, but I swear it's true."

Andreas stared back up the road. "After what we just saw, I'll believe anything. Tell me."

And Parley told him what had happened since he left Ambercrest with Bert's letter. The other soldiers dismounted and gathered close to listen. When Parley reached the part about encountering the Dwergh, the soldiers whispered to one another in alarm.

"Dwergh!"

"It's true, the Dwergh are here!"

"Yes, they're here," Parley said. "But not to steal the gold and gems from our land. They came to help." He told them the true reason the Dwergh had returned, how Bert's letter had finally revealed where the wicked object they sought was hidden, and how Bert was now almost certainly under its spell. All the while Andreas fixed a piercing stare on Parley. The courier began to feel unnerved.

When Parley was done, Andreas spoke. "That's quite a tale, Parley. Now will you tell me why your eyes—er, *eye*—keeps turning to the forest behind me?"

Parley gulped. *You'd never be much of a spy*, he chided himself. *Your face is an open book. An open, ugly book.*

"Well," he said, "remember I mentioned that the Dwergh are here to help? As a matter of fact . . ." He paused, afraid for his hidden friend. But Harth had no such fear. He stepped out from the shadows of the trees and into the sunlight, planted his feet wide, and stood with his hands clasped behind his broad back.

There were shouts of surprise and anger and a chorus of scraping metal as swords were drawn and raised. The soldiers were about to rush the Dwergh, but Andreas sprang to his feet and called out: "Hold! All of you! Stay where you are!"

Andreas stepped toward the Dwergh with his sword still in its sheath. Harth didn't move except to crane his neck to look at the tall knight. Parley was reminded again of how short but wide the Dwergh were, practically square. Harth's head barely came to Andreas's chest, but he was even broader across the shoulders.

"Andreas, this is Harth," Parley said. "He's a Dwergh. But I suppose you worked that out for yourself. He wants to help. It's too late for Will, but maybe Bert can still be saved. Talk to him, Andreas. He has a plan."

Andreas looked down at the Dwergh. "If I talk to you, I risk being accused of treason."

Harth looked up impassively. "And if you don't, you risk suffering and death for your people. Which is the worse evil?"

Andreas pursed his lips and nodded. "Are there more of your folk nearby?"

"Not close," the Dwergh said. "They hide elsewhere. Waiting."

"Waiting for what?"

Harth folded his arms across his chest. "Waiting for your baron to do his part. So they can do theirs."

34

Bert had searched practically the entire castle for his uncle. He wasn't on the walls, despite what the mirror said. A guard in a watchtower told him that Lord Charmaigne had gone down to the courtyard a while ago. But when Bert ran there, a servant told him that his uncle went into the keep. Bert hurried back inside, calling for him, growing more red-faced by the minute. He had to find him before Will showed up. His uncle's men must be told to seize the traitor the moment he arrived.

On the terrace, maybe, talking to his wife, Bert thought. He rushed up the stairs. He didn't understand why his uncle was wandering around. Since he'd slipped him the potion, Uncle Hugh hardly made a move without asking for approval. Bert even had to tell him when to go to sleep.

Aunt Elaine was on the terrace alone, plucking dead flowers off a plant. She looked over with dread when she saw Bert running toward her. It was the same look she always gave him lately.

"Where's Uncle Hugh?" Bert demanded when he was still many steps away.

Aunt Elaine tossed the shriveled blossoms into a bowl

and put her fists on her hips. "We have to talk, Nephew. What's the matter with you lately? And what's going on with you and your uncle? I don't understand it. Once Hugh despised the sight of you. Now I see you whispering to him, and him nodding . . ."

"Just tell me where he is!" Bert shouted. He snatched up the plant and hurled it off the balcony. A second later he heard the satisfying smash of the ceramic pot in the courtyard below. He lowered his head and glared at his aunt. He wanted to tell her that he could have her put in chains if he wanted. But it wasn't time to show everyone who was really in command. *Soon. But not yet.*

Her face went pale as she stared at him. "I haven't seen him," she said, barely opening her mouth to speak. "Please, Bert. Talk to me. You're not—"

"Why didn't you just say that in the first place, you fool!" he said. He whirled and raced back into the keep.

Where could his uncle be? An answer finally occurred to him—and it made so much sense that he chuckled, knowing it must be true. *Of course. He's back in the secret place. Looking for me, while I look for him.* He ran to his room and into the Tunnel of Stars. There was a dim light at the bottom of the stairs. *Yes, Uncle Hugh must be there.*

When he reached the chamber, he saw his uncle sitting in front of the mirror. Bert felt a flash of red-hot anger. "Get away from my throne," he said. "I have something important for you to do."

"And what is that?" his uncle said without turning.

His fingertips scratched the arms of the chair.

Bert saw movement in the shadows of the inner chamber. The beasts had returned. One by one they emerged from the dark opening—the secret path that ended in a hidden crevice, somewhere on the ledge to the north of The Crags. They loped toward Uncle Hugh except for one that limped on an injured leg. The creatures were bigger and more horrific than ever, as if they were still sprouting more terrible spikes and knobs of bone all over their bodies. Their lips curled back and quivered as they glared sideways at Bert, and they left a trail of foaming slobber wherever they walked.

Bert pointed at the beasts. "Your dogs are back, but they failed. Now my brother is coming here."

"I know," said Uncle Hugh. He still hadn't turned.

"What do you mean, you *know?*" Bert screamed. He staggered back, suddenly aware that something was horribly wrong. How could his uncle know what happened . . . unless . . .

"The mirror told me," Uncle Hugh said. He stood and turned to face Bert at last. His mouth was twisted into an ugly smile. The vacant expression was gone from his eyes, replaced by a crafty, narrow glare.

"Told *you?*" Bert put his fingers to his throat. They were shaking. "But the mirror only talks to me. . . ."

"Not anymore," Uncle Hugh said. "Now it's mine."

Bert made a choking sound. He looked past his uncle, at the mirror. "Mirror!" he shouted. His eyes felt warm.

"Talk to me! Tell him you're mine! I found you, not him!" He rushed at it. He wanted to seize it by the frame and run. But his uncle snatched Bert's wrist and jerked him back. Bert wailed and his legs went limp, but Uncle Hugh held him up by the arm. Pain flared in the brutal grip, and only the tips of Bert's shoes scraped the ground.

"You're a stupid, spoiled, little toad, you know that?" Lord Charmaigne said, sneering down at him. "That's why the mirror cast you aside for me. Did you think that potion you slipped me would last forever? Of course not. It wore off, and the mirror didn't bother to tell you it was happening. Do you know why? Because I'm more worthy than a child like you. I can use its power better. And the mirror knows it!"

Bert howled like an animal in a trap. Uncle Hugh just laughed at him and dragged him past the snarling beasts into the inner chamber, to a chain that was attached to the wall. Bert thrashed and kicked, but Uncle Hugh was too strong. He seized one of Bert's ankles and clamped a shackle around it.

"There!" he said, stepping away from Bert's flailing arms and legs. He scratched his chin and furrowed his brow. "Should I keep you alive? Maybe, maybe not. I might need you to lure your father. . . . I'll decide soon enough. See how you do without food or drink for a few days!"

Bert looked around for anything to throw, anything to

use to hurt his uncle. There was nothing but bare stone. "I hate you!" he screamed, and the walls of the chamber answered a dozen times.

Hugh Charmaigne laughed. "And I've always hated you. But I suppose I should thank you, really. For the gift of the mirror. The gift that will help me rule this land. *Every* land!" He grinned as Bert wailed and pounded the ground with his hands and feet.

"Don't be so upset, boy. You'll have company soon enough. I'll bring your cowardly brother down as soon as he arrives. Then I'll choose which one of you I'll need. And feed the other to my dogs."

Will rode with his arms locked around the hunter's waist. He nearly bounced off a dozen times until Gunther, finally confident that they'd left the beast far behind, agreed to slow his horse. And the ride was easier once they climbed onto the road.

Will looked behind them. Half of him was afraid to see more of those monsters in pursuit. The other half hoped to see Andreas and the others charging his way. But the road was empty.

A few minutes later he saw The Crags. It was vaguely familiar, like a half-remembered dream. And now, looking at its foreboding walls in the gloomy shadow of the mountain, he could see why he'd been afraid years before.

"I can't breathe," Gunther croaked.

"Sorry," Will said. At the first sight of the dark castle, he'd tightened his grip around the hunter's waist without realizing it. He loosened his hold.

"Much appreciated," Gunther said after a deep breath. "Well, I'm glad we made it. But that's it for me—I'll never hunt in that valley again, even if Lord Charmaigne flogs me."

They trotted to the gate where a pair of surly guards blocked their path. Will leaned out from behind Gunther, so the two could see him.

"That's the baron's boy," one said to the other. "Master Bert, what were you doing out there?"

Will dismounted. "I'm not Bert, I'm his brother, Will. Listen, we were attacked on the Cliff Road. There were men with me who may be hurt. . . ."

A deep voice called down from the wall above the gate. "You there! Is that the baron's other son?"

The guards looked up. "Yes, it is, Brocuff," one called.

"Good," Brocuff said. He leaned out with a keen stare fixed on Will. "Keep him right there. Lord Charmaigne said he'd be coming."

Will looked up and saw the big, deep-voiced man vanish from sight. He heard boots on stairs on the other side of the wall. This was strange. *How could Uncle Hugh be expecting me?* Sure, he'd been invited to come, but no courier was sent ahead to announce their arrival. There was no way to know he was coming, unless . . . "Did any of our party get here before me? Has the knight, Andreas, been here?"

"Haven't seen nobody but you," said one of the guards. The two of them came toward Will and stood on either side.

"Then how did Uncle—I mean, Lord Charmaigne—know I was coming?" Will was getting an unsettled feeling. The hair on his arms tingled.

Brocuff stepped through the gate. Will had the urge to turn and run. Something was very wrong. But before he could make up his mind, a powerful hand clamped onto his shoulder.

"Come with me," Brocuff rumbled, pulling Will through the gate and into the courtyard.

Will tried to push the hand away. "What are you doing? You don't need to drag me!"

"I was told to bring you directly to Lord Charmaigne," Brocuff said, squeezing even tighter.

"You can't drag me! I'm the baron's son! Let go of me!" Will said, his voice rising. He pried at the fingers, but couldn't even bend the little one back. The door to the keep was ahead, a black rectangle that looked like an open grave, standing on end. Will was sure that if he went into that dark space, he'd never come out. He punched at the hand that held him, and twisted his body, trying to break free. Brocuff pushed Will in front of him, grabbing both shoulders from behind. The black space came closer. "Stop!" Will cried.

Then a familiar figure stepped through the doorway and into the light.

"Let him go now, Brocuff," said Aunt Elaine.

Will stared at her. His heart was pounding, his breath wheezing. He couldn't read her expression. She smiled serenely at the man who still had him in an iron grip.

Brocuff's thick jaw slid from side to side. "I was told to

bring the boy straight to Lord Charmaigne . . . and make sure he didn't . . ."

"Yes, and now my husband wishes me to take him," she said. "Surely you won't defy his orders? You know how he feels about disobedience." There was an edge to her voice, a hint of thorns among the flowers. Brocuff cleared his throat. The fingers loosened a bit on Will's shoulders.

Aunt Elaine smiled at Will. "Nephew, you'll come with me to see your uncle, won't you?" She held out her hand.

Will caught something in her expression. A subtle widening of the eyes, a lift of the brow, a flare of her nostrils. "Of course, Aunt Elaine," he said. Brocuff's grip weakened, and Will shrugged out of it and took her hand.

"Thank you, Brocuff," Aunt Elaine said. She pulled Will inside and pushed the heavy wooden door closed behind them. There was a thick iron bolt on the other side, and she slid it into place and looked furtively around the great hall that they'd entered. The pleasant smile was gone, and her mouth was closed in a pale, grim line. Before Will could ask what was happening, she tapped a finger against her lips and led him into a narrow corridor.

"Not a word now," she whispered. "No one must see or hear us. I have to get you out of here."

"But where's my brother?" Will hissed back.

"Hush!" she said. "Just do exactly as I say!"

*　*　*

They slipped down the dank passage and out into a shadowy corner of the courtyard, close to where the wall of The Crags met the steep mountain. The moment they stepped outside they heard angry shouts. Will couldn't make out the words, but he knew his disappearance must have been the root of the commotion. He heard the thump of boots, getting louder. Aunt Elaine pressed her back to the wall and put her hand across his chest to push him back as well. Will saw a long shadow draw near, and then move away.

He heard his aunt exhale gratefully. "Now," she said, and she pulled him behind her and ran. Will didn't know where they could possibly be going. It looked like they were heading for a sheer, impenetrable face of rock. But then he saw the narrow stairs that had been hacked out of the ledge, three feet wide at the most, leading to the top of the wall.

"Keep low," Aunt Elaine said, pushing him ahead of her. Will climbed the steps on all fours. Near the top he poked his head out and peered into the courtyard. He recognized his uncle, sending men off in every direction as others ran up and reported to him. Uncle Hugh abruptly smacked himself on his head with the heel of his hand. He turned and raced into the keep as if there was a fire inside that needed putting out. *Strange*, Will thought. *What did he just remember?*

Will and his aunt reached the top of the wall. "Over

there," she said, pointing to the nearest watchtower. A grizzled watchman, the oldest fellow Will had seen so far at The Crags, was inside. He gave Will a suspicious glance, but nodded to Aunt Elaine. Will saw beads of sweat on the man's brow.

"Hurry," the watchman said, waving them inside the tower. There was a coiled rope in his hand. "I don't think you have long."

"Thank you, Tristan," Aunt Elaine said. Tristan tied one end of the rope to an iron ring that was secured to the wall. He tossed the coil over.

"Are you sure you can you make it down?" Tristan asked her.

"I don't see why not," Aunt Elaine said. She swung her legs over, wrapped them around the rope, and began to lower herself to the ground, some thirty feet below.

Will looked up at Tristan. This whole episode had his head spinning, but he could tell this man was taking a great risk by helping him. "Thank you," he said.

"I'm doing it for her, lad," Tristan whispered back, jutting his chin toward the place where Aunt Elaine had disappeared. "My arm would've rotted off if it wasn't for that angel's medicine. Of course, you can always put in a good word for me with the baron." He looked over the wall. "She's made it. Down you go."

Will was beside his aunt a moment later. "Follow," she said. She led him along the foot of the mountain, away from The Crags. They went down a gully filled with loose stones, crouching low to stay out of sight. Will was bursting with questions. *Why am I in danger? Where's my brother?* But he knew it wasn't safe to talk yet.

At the bottom of the gully a soldier stood holding the reins of two horses. There was something familiar about him, and Will realized that he looked like a younger version of the watchman they'd just met, with the same round face, small eyes, and upturned nose.

"I can't thank you enough, Thurstan," Aunt Elaine said. "You and your father have fine hearts."

"Not as fine as yours," Thurstan said, flashing a nervous smile.

There was a blue cloak draped over the smaller horse. It looked like something a woman would wear. Aunt Elaine handed it to Will. "Put this on," she said. "If we're seen, they'll think you're my servant."

Thurstan spoke quietly as they mounted their horses. "Be careful, dear lady. We saw some strange beasts on the northern ledge early this morning—right over there."

Will straightened in his saddle. "The beasts were here?"

Thurstan peered up curiously. "That's right, lad. A whole pack of them," he said. His neck craned forward as he looked closely at Will. "Say, you look just like your twin. But that's the point of twins, ain't it?"

"You've seen Bert! Is he all right?" Will asked breathlessly. Thurstan opened his mouth to speak, but closed it again after a glance at Aunt Elaine.

"There's no time, Will," Aunt Elaine said, tugging her reins to guide her horse.

"You'll let the baron know I helped, won't you lad? Put in a word for me?" Thurstan said as Will trotted away.

Will waved feebly. He gnawed on his upper lip as he stared at his aunt. *You still haven't told me where my brother is!*

CHAPTER

36

Bert peered at every link of the chain. He tugged at the metal plate that secured it to the stone wall. He pried at the shackle around his ankle. It was no use. He was trapped.

A strange feeling came over him as if his brain had turned to water and sloshed inside his skull. It made him so dizzy that he lowered himself to the floor, so he wouldn't faint and crack his head. A grinding pain flared behind his eyes, and he felt like he was boiling from the inside out. Sweat erupted all over his body, soaking his clothes and leaving him as wet as if he'd been lying in a tub. He'd felt something like this once before, when he'd been ill—and Will was sick with him, of course—and a terrible fever had finally broken.

And then he began to shiver. He hugged himself and tucked his knees against his chest. The chamber felt cold as ice.

"Mirror, what's wrong with me?" he moaned. "What have you done to me?" But he knew what it had done. It had cast him aside. Betrayed him. The mirror might have been lost forever if not for him. But it only befriended him, until it discovered someone more useful.

He heard the inner voice again, the one the mirror crushed. It was still weak, but getting stronger. *Bert, what have you been up to? Don't you realize what you've done?*

And then, as if he was waking from a dream, he remembered exactly what he'd done while in the mirror's thrall. He opened his mouth wide, but the horror was so great he couldn't even scream. He rolled onto his stomach and clenched his hands onto the back of his head.

"Will," he gasped. He'd created those monsters and sent them after his brother. By some miracle Will had gotten away, but now he was coming here, right into his uncle's grasping hands. And when Will arrived, one of them would die.

It should be me, Bert thought.

The beasts were resting in a protective circle around the mirror. The nearest one turned a frosted eye toward Bert. Its tongue slithered sideways across the jumble of jagged teeth. A low growl issued from somewhere deep in its throat.

"W-W-Why did I do all those things?" Bert said through chattering teeth. "Mirror, why d-did you make me do it?"

He didn't expect a response. But the surface of the mirror shimmered and clouded. It was like staring into a fog. He saw a dark form nearing the surface. It had done this before, but always stopped before fully revealing itself. This time the form approached until only a thin, transparent veil of mist covered it.

The thing was shaped like a face and had the color of bruised and rotting flesh. It filled the mirror from top to bottom, as big as a shield, and it was mounted on the end of a long jointed neck that vanished into the depths of the glass. At first Bert saw no features at all—no mouth, no nose, no eyes. Then there *were* eyes—fist-size, lidless eyes, at least five of them, popping up all over the face, and then sinking in again, like onions in a boiling soup. The strange skin bubbled and shifted and squirmed with a sickening oozy sound. Bert was on the verge of understanding why it moved liked that—what the skin was *made* of—but he didn't want to know. He threw his arm across his face to block the sight.

Why now? he thought. *Why didn't you show me your real face until now?* But it was obvious: The mirror fooled him from the start, never revealing its true self. But now that it didn't need him anymore, it was pleased to show its face. Bert's shivers grew worse, but it wasn't just from the chills.

The mirror spoke. *I did not make you do those things, Bertram. Don't you understand? I only helped you pursue what you really wanted.* The voice was different now. Before it was reassuring, loving. Now it dripped with cold contempt. It mocked him.

"No, never! I'd never hurt my brother!" Bert cried.

Those things were in your heart. In your soul.

"No—you put them there!"

You can tell yourself that if you want. But it doesn't matter. Now your heart and soul are mine, the mirror said. *Like the others.*

My soul? Others? Bert dared to peek out over the top of his arm. He wished he hadn't. Now the awful face was crystal clear. The skin moved, because it was covered with tiny, writhing worms. No, not covered with them; the skin was *made* of those things. And as Bert stared, transfixed by horror, the maggoty things wriggled away from the middle of the face, leaving a gaping mouth hole behind. Bert glimpsed transparent figures inside the throat, and heard unearthly moans. *Ghosts!* It was hard to tell one from the other, the way they faded and blurred together, but they looked like ancient, burly men with long flowing beards. They swam toward the opening with vaporous arms reaching out as if they might escape that maw. But before they reached the surface, the worms wriggled in again. The mouth shrank and closed, leaving a thin, curving smile for a moment before even that was completely erased.

Bert's mind went numb. He wished he would faint. That would be merciful. He rolled onto his side and put his back to the mirror.

He saw one of the beasts cowering against the wall nearby. Even those vile creatures had slunk away from the face of the mirror. Bert heard them whine and saw them look toward the Tunnel of Stars. He heard footfalls on the steps. And his uncle's words haunted his ears.

I'll bring your cowardly brother down as soon as he arrives. Then I'll choose which one of you I'll need, and feed the other to my dogs.

His heart twisted inside his chest as the steps descended. And then his uncle came in alone. Lord Charmaigne strode across the chamber, muttering furiously.

Bert seized his chance. "Look at the mirror, Uncle Hugh! Look at the face! Don't you see? The mirror isn't your friend, it's a—"

"Quiet!" his uncle snapped, putting a hand on the hilt of his sword. "That brother of yours is a slippery rat. But I can find him. Wherever he hides." Uncle Hugh took another stride and stood before the mirror.

He'll see the face! Bert thought. *Then he'll understand.* But he cried aloud when he saw that the demon face had vanished, and the mirror's surface shimmered handsomely once more.

"Mirror," Uncle Hugh said. "There's something I must know."

Aunt Elaine finally slowed so their horses could rest, just as they entered a forest of birch. Will stopped beside her, aching to know what was wrong with his brother. But before he could ask, he heard the sound of pursuit. Horses, pounding the earth. A man shouted orders in the distance.

His aunt's head turned and her face went pale. "What? I don't understand—we weren't seen! How could they know?" She bit her lip. Then a fierce look came to her eyes. "Come on, Will!" She kicked at the side of her horse and rode swiftly into the trees.

Will followed. He looked over the tops of the trees at a high cliff that curved around the forest on either side, and wondered why his aunt led them into a place with no escape. *More bad terrain!*

The horses galloped at a reckless pace, threading between the trees. Branches slapped his face and chest. He raised a forearm to shield his eyes. The jutting limb of one birch nearly unseated his aunt—she teetered perilously, one arm flailing, before she regained her balance. Will shot a look over his shoulder and saw men on horses closing in behind—better, faster riders than his aunt and himself. They were soldiers from The Crags— eight, maybe ten of them.

The nearest had already drawn his sword. He was close enough for Will to recognize. Brocuff bellowed after them: "Stop in the name of Lord Charmaigne!"

"They're going to catch us!" Will shouted to his aunt. She veered right suddenly, and Will pulled hard on his reins to make his horse follow. They burst into a grassy clearing with the cliff looming overhead. Will was sur- prised to see a low stone cottage in an open meadow before them.

His aunt was already off her horse, running into the tiny building. Will leaped down to follow, just as the mounted soldiers thundered into the clearing. Brocuff rode in front of Will to cut him off from the cottage. The horse reared up as Brocuff pulled back on the reins, and Will darted under the animal's neck. He felt fingers grasp at his cloak and swatted the hand away. Behind he heard the thump of boots on the grass.

Will ran into the open doorway. If there had been a door to slam behind him, he would have shut it. *What good does this do us?* he wondered, looking around the strange little place, with tiny rooms and a ceiling so low anyone bigger than him would have to stoop. There were footsteps close behind him.

"Here, Will!" his aunt cried. Will saw her head sticking out of a hole in the floor. *A trap door!* He ran to it as she ducked out of sight. He didn't wait to see if there was a ladder or steps. He simply jumped in and landed on his feet and fingertips, just a few feet below. From the scant light that fell through the opening, Will could see that he'd dropped into a tunnel. His aunt was in front of him, and she seized his hand and pulled him into the dark passage.

Voices from above shouted. "Where are they?"

"Check the other rooms!"

"Hey, there's a hole in the floor!"

Will and his aunt made slow progress in the pitch-black tunnel—slow because it was too dark to see, and because they tried to be stealthy. Will looked back at the opening. He saw one of the soldier's heads come down through the trap door and stare his way. But he didn't think the man could see him. *Can't even see my own feet,* he thought.

The voices of the men carried easily down the tunnel.

"What's in there?"

"Can't see a blessed thing, Brocuff! It's blacker than coal!"

"Blasted Dwergh rat hole! Well, you have to follow them!"

"What, and get knifed in the dark? Why don't *you* go down there, you're so eager?"

"Because I'm in charge, imbecile! You want to tell Lord Charmaigne we lost him?"

"I don't want to tell Lord Charmaigne anything.

There's something wrong with him, if you ask me. He has the same look in his eye the baron's nephew got . . ."

The voices faded just as they started to say something Will needed to hear. He stopped and tugged on his aunt's hand.

"No!" she whispered. "We have to keep moving. There's only one way to go. We don't want them catching up, do we?"

She didn't say another word. She just pulled on his hand, and Will followed. He only heard one more thing that was said behind them. It was Brocuff's deep, blustering voice. "What are you waiting for? Light a torch!"

CHAPTER

38

The lightless tunnel was just wide enough for them to walk side by side. There were no turns, no other corridors, no passages to the surface. Aunt Elaine wouldn't let Will talk at all, so the questions kept burning in his mind. He thought he might scream if he couldn't ask them soon.

The ceiling was low—just over his head—with even lower crossbeams. Will kept one hand in front of him and one on the ceiling, so he wouldn't smack his head on those fat timbers. For a while damp, stringy matter hung down and brushed his hands and face. *Roots*, he figured. But then that stuff was gone, and the earthy, humid smell turned cool and dry. There were no more wooden supports—the tunnel was bored into solid rock.

Will tried to remember which direction the passage had led. In the chaos of the chase, he hadn't paid much attention. But he thought they were headed straight for the mountain. *And now we're under it*, he thought just as his outstretched hand touched a solid wall.

"Is this the end?" Will asked quietly.

"No," Aunt Elaine whispered. "There's a door in this

wall. But it has to be opened. I just need to . . . Yes, here it is."

"Here *what* is?" Will asked. The answer came in a groan of metal that rose and fell in pitch, and was followed by a deep, sonorous clang that made him jump.

"What was that?" he said.

"The knocker," she replied.

"Knocker? You mean someone's in there?"

"I certainly hope so," Aunt Elaine said. Will heard that rusty screech, followed by another deep clang, four more times. Then a pause, and two more. He pictured something like a door knocker, but bigger, striking a bell embedded in the stone. When he touched the wall he could feel the vibrations. *I guess we don't have to be quiet anymore.*

Will pulled off the servant's cloak and threw it aside. "Aunt Elaine, tell me what's happened to Bert," he said. He heard her sigh deeply. And then she answered him.

"I don't really know," she said. "We got along so well at first. But then a strange transformation came over him, and he stopped talking to me. He became angry. Secretive. There was a frightening look in his eyes, as if he wasn't really himself anymore. He'd vanish for hours and suddenly reappear. Then something even stranger happened. My husband became his puppet. Your brother would order him around like a slave, and Hugh would obey! You'd have to know your uncle to realize how ludicrous that is. He's a cruel and arrogant bully. He doesn't take orders from anyone.

"Well, I had to find out what was going on. But they were both so stealthy that I couldn't get near them. Until just a few hours ago—when Bert was in a rage, looking for your uncle. I followed him to his room and saw him go through a secret door that led to a long flight of stairs. I don't know where the stairs ended. I didn't go down all the way, because I heard a dreadful snarling and snapping, as if something horrible was below. So I stayed put and listened. I heard your brother and your uncle talk about you. They said you were coming to—" Aunt Elaine cut herself off with a gasp. "Look!" she cried.

Will turned to look the way they'd come. All was dark except for a tiny rectangle of orange, growing fast.

"It's them," he said. He heard a whisper of cloth nearby and reached out. He found her hand and clasped it.

The glow had already doubled in size. Will saw torches and the dark shapes of men, hunched over and loping toward them.

"Will, you've been very brave," Aunt Elaine said. She squeezed his hand.

"There they are!" Brocuff shouted, now that the torchlight was near. The men broke into a run, as fast as they could under the low ceiling. Their weapons were drawn, flashing yellow when the blades caught the light. Will wished he had his knife, his sword, anything. Aunt Elaine put a hand across his chest and pushed him behind her.

Will was about to object when he heard a grinding noise. A thick slab in the middle of the stone barrier was rising. And in the narrow gap below, he saw more light—coming from the other side.

"Will, go under! *Now!*" his aunt shouted, pushing him down. Will dropped onto his stomach and crawled under the slowly rising stone.

"Come on!" he screamed to his aunt. She was right behind him. Ahead of him, beyond the slab, he saw a pair of boots. A thick hand reached down, and he took it, feeling rough skin against his palm. He was pulled through, and he spun back on his hands and knees to help his aunt. She looked at him and smiled fiercely, and he grabbed her outstretched hand. He pulled. Everything but her legs had come through. "I've got you!" he said. And then someone tugged much harder from the other side.

She kicked and thrashed, trying to free herself, but was drawn back under the slab. Will held fast to her hand and was dragged back with her.

Aunt Elaine twisted her hand and wrenched it free from his. "Lower it," she shouted past Will. "Save the boy!"

"No! We have to help her," Will snapped. He didn't see who raised the door until he turned his head. His mind reeled as he saw a short, wide, brawny being with a sprawling black beard. *A Dwergh!* Will was stunned for a moment—long enough for the chain on the wheel behind the Dwergh to unwind. The slab of rock boomed down, shearing off his aunt's pleas to save him.

A cloud of dust billowed up, and he choked on it. He scrambled to his feet and gaped at the stranger. It was a Dwergh; there could be no mistake. The Dwergh's broad ax leaned against the wall of the passage, and his lantern hung from a hook in the wall.

"How could you let them take her!" he shouted. He rushed at the Dwergh and tried to punch him, but the Dwergh caught him by the wrist.

The Dwergh growled out harsh words. "Holtokh! *Ang rekhush!*"

"Let go of me!" Will shouted. With his other hand he grabbed the Dwergh's beard and pulled. The Dwergh's expression—what Will could see within that dense beard, anyway—filled with fury. The Dwergh grabbed his arm and squeezed, and Will cried out in pain.

"Never grab a Dwergh by the beard," a gruff voice said in a strange accent. "If you want to keep your hand attached to your arm, that is." It was another Dwergh, coming down the tunnel. An older one with silver hair. Will loosened his grip, and the first Dwergh shoved him away and spat on the floor.

The old Dwergh stopped in front of him. He panted, and his beard rose and fell like bellows. "How did you know about this place?"

"I didn't," Will cried. "My aunt brought me here. But those men took her! We have to—"

"Your *aunt?*" the old Dwergh cried. He talked rapidly with the first Dwergh in their odd language. The old Dwergh's face grew even grimmer. Finally he turned back to Will.

"I Iamokh says there were too many to fight. Nothing could be done."

"But we can't just—"

"Please, young man," the old Dwergh said. "Dwergh do not fear battles, but we know when to choose them. Hamokh is one of our bravest. If he could have helped Elaine, he would have."

Will blinked. "You . . . you know my aunt?"

The old Dwergh bowed. "And now tell me, though I think I know, which of the baron's sons are you?"

Will slid his hands over the top of his head and down across his face. This day was full of surprises: some strange, some horrible, some unfathomable. And everything was backward. He stood before the kingdom's fiercest enemy, who just saved him from his uncle's soldiers—the very men who ought to protect him! Friends were foes, foes were friends, a family castle was a death trap and the enemy's lair was a sanctuary. He was so bewildered he could barely answer the question. "I'm Will Charmaigne. But how do you know all this?"

Before the Dwergh could answer, a clanging burst out, many times louder on this side of the door. Will clapped his hands over his ears. He looked toward the source of the sound and saw an enormous iron flower the size of a barrel sticking out of the wall. The ringing echoed down the length of the tunnel before them.

"It's her—she must have gotten away!" Will shouted over the noise. "Open the door!"

The old Dwergh shook his head. "It is the men, trying to fool us," he called out in return. "They do not know the sequence I taught Elaine." The ringing died away. The Dwergh laid a heavy hand on Will's shoulder. "Come with us, Will Charmaigne. For now, we can only hope your aunt will be all right. She will survive, if that is the will of the earth. There are many things I have to tell you. But we have to get you to a safe place, where the mirror cannot see you."

"Mirror?" Will said. "See me? I . . . I don't understand."

"I know. I will help you understand," said the Dwergh. "My name is Kholl. And we share another friend, by the name of Par Lee."

39

Bert was still cold, and his mouth was dry as dust. Thirst would be the end of him, he knew, long before hunger. A few days; that was as long as a person could go without water. Someone told him that once.

As he lay on his back on the floor of the chamber and stared at the daggers of stone above, he heard a quiet sound, not far away. It was almost lost amid the occasional flap of leathery wings as bats flew from place to place overhead, or out through the crack in the wall of the chamber. It was a tiny, wet *splat*.

He cocked his ear and waited. It was nearly a minute before he heard it again. *Splat.* Somewhere to his right. *Water dripping from the ceiling,* he thought. It might be close enough to reach.

He looked at the mirror. Its surface shined with a duller light than usual. He didn't know if the thing inside the mirror was still aware when the glass looked like that. Perhaps it was sleeping. Or maybe it never rested, and watched him even now.

The beasts had returned to guard the mirror after the face disappeared. As they slept around it in a circle, they

whined and chuffed. Groaning, stretching sounds issued
from under their hides. Some of them had sprouted
sharp horns above their eyes or beside their snouts. And
the spikes of bone along their spines looked longer than
ever. *They're still growing*, Bert realized.

He inched toward where he thought the drops of
water were falling, using his elbows and shoulder blades
to wriggle along as quietly as possible. The chain clinked
softly as it stretched out in his wake. Bert heard another
splat not far away. He slid forward some more, and his
head touched a low mound of rock. The next drop of
water landed on his forehead, and he gasped aloud. He
edged forward a little more, propped the back of his
head on the stone mound, and opened his mouth. And
waited.

And waited.

And then a fat drop of cool water exploded on his
tongue and trickled down his throat. The taste was clean
and sharp. As he waited for more drops and the slow
relief of his thirst, he thought about Will and hoped his
brother had gotten away safely. But how could Will ever
really escape as long as the mirror could reveal to Uncle
Hugh where he'd gone? There was only one way that
Bert could imagine. It was what he would do if he ever
managed to get away.

Run, Will. Keep running. Never stop running.

40

"You must put this on," said Kholl. He held up a thick chain with two hands, so Will could slip it over his neck. Hanging from the chain was a silver disk studded with glittering red and green stones around the edge. It was large enough to cover Will's palm as he looked at the strange writing engraved in a spiral on its surface.

Will's head spun from everything he learned these past few hours. Now he wondered why it was so important to wear this thing. He looked at Kholl with one eye squinting.

"This amulet once belonged to a mighty Dwergh sorcerer," the old Dwergh said, answering the unspoken question. "We have kept it with us all this time, in case of need. It will shield you, and those who stay near you, from the sight of the mirror. And since it is you the mirror has already tried to destroy, you must be the one to wear it."

Will ducked his head through the chain. He was still getting accustomed to the idea of this Ulgonog: a demon trapped inside a mirror, who could see him wherever he went. A demon that turned his own brother against him. A demon that existed only to breed misery, and feast on the souls it corrupted. And he'd learned another astounding thing: Years ago Aunt Elaine encountered the Dwergh while searching for rare plants in the mountains behind The Crags. She'd befriended them, and even helped them with her medicines.

And besides all those uncanny developments, there was also the little stone creature with bulging diamond eyes that followed the Dwergh wherever they went, handled many of their chores, and was fed a steady diet of red-hot coals to keep it animated.

Will would have been more confounded by all this if he wasn't so worried. "What do we do now?" he said to the silver-bearded Dwergh, the only one there who shared his language.

"We wait, until Par Lee and Harth return. To tell us if your father will help us."

CHAPTER

41

It was a dim sensation at first, not enough to rouse him from the cold pit of sleep into which he'd tumbled. But Bert finally became conscious of icy stone pressed against the side of his face, and a whispery voice that called his name. He fought awareness. Even the terrible dreams that stalked his sleep were better than the real nightmare that awaited.

The voice of the mirror pried into his skull.

Bertram. Turn your eyes to me, it said.

"No," he mumbled, knowing it didn't matter. There was no resisting the voice's command. He hated the mirror for what he'd done under its spell. And he hated himself because, in his heart, he wanted the mirror back. He longed for its magic to be his again. And so he was powerless against it. He lifted his head. When he saw the appalling face again, sour bile erupted in his throat and stung the back of his tongue.

The face hovered on the end of that long, segmented neck. The mass of worms bulged here and there, and the lidless eyes bobbed up and stared at him, quivering.

Bert's stomach lurched at the awful wet sounds. *Slither.*
Squish. Slurp.

Do you know what I feed on, Bertram? Do you know what
sustains me? the mirror asked.

"Leave me alone," Bert said. He squeezed his eyes
closed. "Please."

Souls, replied the mirror. *Souls are my nectar.* Bert's eyes
opened against his will. The mouth was back, a gaping
funnel. The throat was infested with more of the wormy
things, and they stretched and crooked like a thousand
beckoning fingers. Bert felt a strange sensation as if
something tugged at things beneath his skin. Prickly
pain erupted on his forehead, his chest, the palms of his
hands—*everywhere.* He gasped, and he would have
screamed, but for the moment he couldn't breathe. His
vision darkened, his ears filled with a windy roar, and his
fingers went numb. The only thing he felt keenly was
stinging pain on his hands and chest. He saw sparkling
mist come out of his skin, like vapor off a warm pond on
a cool morning. Tendrils of mist drifted across the
chamber. They touched the surface of the mirror, passed
through it as if the glass wasn't there, and swirled down
the horrible throat.

Very good, the mirror said when it was done. *I will feed*
again soon. Yes, once more may do. The mouth closed, the fat
eyes sank into the wriggling mass, and the face vanished
into the depths of the mirror. The beasts had retreated to

the far corners of the chamber, and they began to slink back.

Bert looked at his palms and saw tiny beads of red where the mist had emerged. He pulled the collar of his shirt out and saw the same dots on his pale chest. He knew the mirror had taken part of him away—devoured him, feasted on him. Like it must have done to others before him, the myriad ghosts he'd seen deep in the thing's throat. He moaned and crawled as far from the mirror as the chain would allow. His head dropped to the floor, and the last thought he had was for his brother.

Run, Will. Keep running.

Bert woke again to the sound of Uncle Hugh cursing and the beasts growling. Someone else was in the chamber now too, besides his uncle—there were muffled, inarticulate cries. His mind was muddled, and he pinched his cheek to try to clear it. He could barely feel the skin clamped between his fingers and thumb. He opened his eyes, but nothing was in focus. Blinking helped.

Uncle Hugh had a woman with him. He had one hand on her arm and the other across her mouth. Bert stared. He knew her. It was Aunt Elaine.

His uncle took his hand off her mouth. "Scream again, and the dogs will have you," he said.

Aunt Elaine staggered back when she saw the pack of beasts licking their teeth at the sight of her. Then her glance fell on Bert.

"Bert . . . is that you? Or is it Will?" she said. Her voice trembled when she spoke. Bert was too dizzy to reply. He lifted a hand, and it fell limply back onto the stone.

"That's your little friend Bert," Uncle Hugh said, mocking her. "I'll have the other whelp soon enough, though. But first I have a special place just for you."

Aunt Elaine tried to shrug out of his grip. "Hugh— there's something wrong with you. Can't you feel it? It's not too late to make things right. You have to let Bert go—look at him, he isn't well. He could be dying. He's your nephew, he shares your blood!"

Uncle Hugh just snorted. "Actually, once I'm sure I don't need him, I think my dogs will share his blood!" A savage look was on his face: a broad toothy smile and scowling eyes. He pulled Elaine toward the inner chamber. She leaned back and pushed with her feet, trying to stop him.

"Why, Hugh? Why would you want to hurt us?"

Uncle Hugh laughed. "Never fret, my dear. I won't harm *you*. I need your herb lore to find the ingredients for my spells. But I'll make a potion for you first—then you'll happily do whatever I tell you." He dragged her across the floor, toward one of the tall boxes that stood on end. He threw the latch and pulled the lid open. A pile of yellow-white bones clattered onto the floor, and a skull tumbled out last. Uncle Hugh swept the bones away with the side of his foot. He shoved Aunt Elaine into the box, slammed the door, and latched it again.

"There now!" he said. He wiped his hand across three red lines on the side of his face, where Aunt Elaine must have scratched him before her hands were tied. "So you won't tell me where that pest escaped to and who helped him? I'll find out anyway, Wife."

Bert watched his uncle walk to the mirror. It felt as if he was watching someone else's nightmare.

"Mirror!" Uncle Hugh shouted. "Where has my nephew Will gone? And who is with them—men or Dwergh?" A familiar ringing rose from the depths of the shining glass. The mirror took a long time before it answered. *I cannot answer. I cannot see.*

Uncle Hugh's mouth hung open. "What do you mean you cannot see? I thought you could see everything!"

I cannot see this. There is a cloak across the boy. Something hides him from my sight.

Bert looked at the mirror. Dark ripples spread across its face. Its voice had always been so cool and silky, so confident. But just then, he thought he'd heard something different. Was it . . . fear?

Uncle Hugh raised his hands. His fingers curled up like a dying flower. His fists shook, and his breath hissed in and out through his teeth. The beasts lifted their horned heads and stared at him.

"If you can't find the boy, then tell me what my

brother is doing!" Uncle Hugh said. He pressed a palm over one eye and clutched his head as if it was aching.

The dark ripples vanished, and the mirror shimmered and rang. The answer came swiftly. *The baron gathers his men in the courtyard of Ambercrest. They prepare to ride to battle. A hundred riders will come to The Crags; hundreds of men on foot will follow.*

Bert wanted to exult at this news. Somehow his father found out what was happening and was riding to the rescue. But Bert felt nothing. His heart and mind were cold and dead. Nothing mattered anymore. The mirror had taken the best of him, drawn it right out of his skin and devoured it. All he could truly feel was sorrow and regret. And one more thing, the last thing he wanted to feel: He was craving—still craving—the mirror.

He watched his uncle practically dance his way out of the chamber and up the stairs. "Oh, dear brother, if you only knew that I can see every move you make. What a trap I'll set for you . . . what a lovely trap . . ."

Uncle Hugh's voice had just faded away when Bert heard his aunt's tremulous call. "Bert! Tell me what's happened. What is this place? What was that voice?"

Bert saw her fingers poke through the eye hole. One of the beasts charged at the box, snarling. She pulled her fingers back as the hideous thing reared up, clawed at the hole, and barked savagely: "*Death! Death!*"

Aunt Elaine didn't make a sound again. Nor did Bert.

42

Will and the Dwergh huddled in the dim light of the caves, near the protection of the amulet.

It would be another day before the baron arrived, if he agreed to help and didn't simply toss Harth into the dungeon. Knowing his father, Will feared he might do just that. Still, just before he left Ambercrest, Will caught a glimpse of something he'd never noticed before: his father's wiser, more understanding nature. Had he seen the true man beneath that belligerent crust?

For now all Will could do was wait. And rest. And talk—with Kholl, anyway. While the rest of the band conversed in their own tongue, dozed, sharpened their axes or mended their armor, Will and the eldest Dwergh spoke about their people, their homes, their families, and their lives.

The more Will learned, the more he felt his hostility and distrust melt away like ice in spring. Kholl showed him how the hair of his ancestors and dearest friends was woven into his own beard, which, it turned out, was why the Dwergh were so touchy about having their beards pulled. He told Will about the great castles of the

Dwergh lords and kings on the far side of the mountains, castles that were half under the ground and half above. He talked about vast, dark lakes under the earth that teemed with blind, glassy fish (the world's most delicious meal, the old Dwergh insisted).

The revelations seemed never-ending. Perhaps the most amazing thing was that Kholl *knew* Snow White. He was among the seven who saved her! And the rest of that brave band was entombed not far away, in a place Kholl promised to show Will one day. "If it all ends well."

Will scraped his bowl clean. He'd never been fond of mushrooms—hated the way they squished between his teeth—but he was so famished that his stomach persuaded his tongue. "I hope we can help Bert," he said. "And I hope Aunt Elaine will be all right."

"If it is the will of the earth, they will survive," Kholl said.

Will dropped his spoon into the bowl. "How much longer will it be, do you think? I can't tell how much time is passing without seeing the sun."

Kholl dug into his thick beard to scratch his chin. "If your friend Par Lee is right, and their horses are swift, it will be soon."

Will's spirits lifted at the thought of seeing Parley again. The old rascal was alive after all. He was still thinking about the courier when a loud ringing echoed through the tunnels. There was a series of clangs: two, then five, then four, then two. Will's head craned up. "That's not the same bell, is it?" he said.

"You have good ears, young Will. That is another entrance. Harth has returned. And your Par Lee with him, I presume. Come—we must all go, and stay close together."

The six Dwergh and Will moved swiftly through the tunnels. The passage turned gradually up until they met a wall of rock with a round, iron door in the middle. Another one of those flower-shaped bells was embedded in the center of the door. The Dwergh hefted their axes and stood at the ready. One of the Dwergh pulled on a lever, and the door swung open. Three lamp-lit figures stood in a cave on the other side—one short and wide, and two much taller.

Will shouted. *"Andreas!"* He dashed through the opening and threw himself at the knight. Andreas dropped his sword, so he wouldn't injure the boy. He caught Will and staggered back, laughing in disbelief. "Will! My boy! You're alive!"

Parley crossed his arms, tapped a foot on the ground, and cleared his throat loudly. "What? No greeting for your old friend, Parley?"

Will pried himself from Andreas and embraced the courier. "Oh, Parley, I *expected* to see you. But I'm just as happy, believe me!"

Parley sniffed. His bottom lip trembled and tears gushed forth, even from his eyeless socket. "We were sure we'd lost you," he wailed. "I nearly died myself when I heard." He leaned over Will's shoulder and blew his nose ferociously on his own sleeve.

Kholl smiled, but when he spoke to the Dwergh that just arrived, his expression turned grave.

"Well, Harth?" Kholl said. Everyone fell still and waited for the answer.

"The baron and his men ride to The Crags as we hoped," Harth said. "This man is Andreas, a knight of their kingdom. He insisted on coming here."

"To keep an eye on us, I suppose," said Kholl.

"The baron trusts you in this matter, if that's what you're getting at," Andreas said. "But I must inform you that he considers this a temporary truce. He will follow the plan as you suggested. Then, whether we fail or succeed, you must return to your mountains immediately, or face the consequences."

"Is that so," said Kholl. His eyes flickered darkly as he stared at Andreas.

Parley raised his hands and patted the air. "Now, those were the baron's words, not this good fellow's. The important thing is, we have a plan. . . ."

Kholl snorted. "So why did you insist on coming, Knight? We didn't ask for another man."

"I came to help save the baron's other son, because I failed to protect this one." Andreas laid a hand on Will's shoulder. "Will, your father wanted to be here himself. But Harth talked him out of it."

"It would have spoiled the plan," said Harth. "The mirror will certainly have its eye on the baron. In fact, we are counting on it."

Will tugged at the knight's sleeve. "Is my father in danger, Andreas?"

"From an enemy that sees every move you make from afar? Of course he is. We all are, Will. We can only hope that your father follows the plan we made—that, in his zeal, he doesn't try to do too much." Andreas noticed the amulet around Will's neck. He reached and held it between his thumb and forefinger. "Harth, is this the charm you told me about?"

"It is," said Harth.

Andreas frowned. "Well. As for us, Will, we can only hope that this trinket you wear is as powerful as our new friends say."

"It had better be. Now, enough talk," said Harth. He said something in the Dwerghish tongue to the rest who stood watching and waiting. Their brows came down fiercely, and their fists tightened around the handles of their weapons. "It is time to act," Harth said. "Let us go!"

They left through the same cave, which opened to a dense wood. It was dark outside—the middle of the night, Parley informed Will. Harth took the lead, and they moved swiftly through the trees. A bright moon, more than half full, was overhead, and they could make their way without lanterns or torches. Will counted ten in the party now—eleven, including Mokh.

"Andreas, what *is* the plan?" Will asked. "What is my father doing?"

"Leading a small force to The Crags," Andreas said.

"But if the mirror knows . . ." Will's voice trailed off.

"We *want* the mirror to know," Andreas said. "Remember the advice of the general of the east, Will: keep your enemy confused and off balance. We know a direct assault on The Crags with only a hundred men would be suicide. But your father's attack will be a feint. Before sunrise he will charge at the main gate, but break off at the last moment. While he draws the attention of the mirror—and the soldiers of The Crags, for that matter—we will run to the ledge at the north end of the wall. It won't be easy to get there unseen. We have to cross open ground between The Crags and the swamp. But in a way we're lucky. There used to be a village at the foot of the ledge, but your uncle burned it down not long ago. So at least no villagers will raise the alarm."

"But why are we going to that ledge at all?" said Will.

Andreas looked around to see how close Harth and Kholl were, and lowered his voice. "Harth had an interesting piece of information for us. Centuries ago, before Snow White ever lived there, The Crags and its lands were given to our kingdom as a peace offering from the

Dwergh. The Crags was *built* by the Dwergh, you see. But apparently the Dwergh neglected to mention that there was a hidden chamber beneath the keep—and a secret way into that chamber from the outside. You can imagine that your father had mixed feelings about this news. He was glad to hear there might be a way to penetrate The Crags and save Bert. But he wasn't pleased that our so-called enemy knew about this vulnerable spot all along—and might have used it in an attack against our people.

"But nevertheless that's precisely what we mean to do. Now, each of these Dwergh seems to have a particular area of knowledge. One of them, named Kortz, knows quite a bit about Dwergh castles. Look behind us, Will. Do you see the tallest Dwergh with one silver band and one gold around his wrist? That's him. Kortz is fairly certain that he can find the hidden entrance on the northern ledges."

"*Fairly* certain," Parley said with a sigh. "That's the trouble with this plan. We're *fairly* certain the baron will give us the diversion we need. We're *fairly* certain we can get to the ledge without being slaughtered. We're *fairly* certain what's-his-name there can find the hidden entrance. And we're *fairly* certain that smashing the mirror will be enough to kill this monstrosity. That's too many *fairly*'s for my taste."

Harth had been a few strides ahead, but he slowed to

allow the three of them to catch up. He slapped Parley on the back. "Never fear, Par Lee. If it is the will of the earth, we will find the mirror and destroy it."

Parley's mouth knotted up. "You Dwergh have good ears."

Bert's muscles quivered as he pushed himself into a seated position and watched his uncle. There was fire under the cauldron, and smoke rose and pooled between the hanging cones of rock. Uncle Hugh consulted the book of spells and potions, and murmured an incantation. He pried open a long-sealed bottle and poured its liquid into the cauldron. Something gurgled and popped, and a thick puff of green smoke billowed high.

His uncle wiped his hands on his shirt and walked to the mirror. He glanced at Bert as he went by. Bert shivered at the cold look in his uncle's eye, the wild, matted hair and the dry white spittle in the corners of his mouth. *Is that how I looked? As mad as that?*

"Mirror," Uncle Hugh said. "Where is my brother now?"

The familiar ring and shimmer came again. *The baron charges with his men at a reckless speed in the dark. He rides ahead, exhorting them. They have had little rest. Just before dawn, they will arrive.*

Uncle Hugh crunched his knuckles and smiled. "Very good. And are they lightly armored?"

Light armor, or none at all, to speed their journey.

Uncle Hugh mumbled happily to himself and peered into the cauldron. He unsheathed the knife at his hip and dipped the blade into whatever simmered inside. A thick, milky liquid dripped off like warm honey. He blew on the blade and carried it to where Bert sat. Crouching low, he waved the knife in front of Bert's face. "Do you know what I've brewed here, Nephew?"

Bert stared at the knife. The thin coat of liquid turned clear as it dried. There was a lump in his throat, and he had to swallow before he could answer. "M-more . . . more of the obedience potion?"

"No, foolish boy. There's time for that later." Uncle Hugh brought the tip of the blade near Bert's nose, almost touching it. "This is *poison*. And what a poison! Why, even the tiniest scratch will bring a slow, painful death. I've brewed a mighty batch, Nephew. A bucketful! And do you know who it's for?"

Bert shook his head and closed his eyes. *Of course I know.*

Uncle Hugh slid the knife into its sheath, careful not to prick himself on the blade. "This is for the man who stole my barony, that's who. The trap is set, Nephew. When the baron nears The Crags, he'll see the gate left open by incompetent soldiers. He'll watch a small group of men run like cowards. That's all the bait your father needs. He'll rush through like the great hero he imagines himself to be, taking the lead as always! And when he charges into the courtyard with his hundred men, *three hundred archers* will surround him—and every arrow will be tipped with my poison. Three hundred arrows, all aimed at one man! Do you think they'll miss?" Uncle Hugh let loose a giddy, high-pitched laugh. His bulging eyes looked like they might pop out of his face.

Aunt Elaine called out from the box in the rear of the chamber, frail and terrified. "Hugh, please. You aren't yourself. It's that voice I heard—it's making you do these things. You have to fight it!"

Uncle Hugh shook with laughter. "Listen, Nephew—did you hear a mouse? Did you hear its little squeak?"

"Listen to her, Uncle Hugh," Bert said. His voice was just a whisper. He couldn't breathe deep enough to make it louder. "There's something wicked inside the mirror. It makes you think it's your friend, but it's not. It lies. It finds your weakness and uses it against you. And when you die, you're trapped inside the mirror. I saw them. I saw the ghosts."

Uncle Hugh's smile melted. "*You're* the liar. You'd say any foolish thing to get the mirror back. But it's *mine*. It wants to be mine. Because it knows how powerful I can become."

Bert shook his head. "No, Uncle Hugh. It will make you do terrible things. The mirror twists everything around. It made me think the people I love were my enemies. I almost killed my brother—and now it wants you to do the same to *your* brother. But you can't!"

Uncle Hugh cast a smoldering glare upon Bert. "Do

you know what it was like when the king gave the barony to my *younger* brother? Can you understand the shame, knowing that everyone was talking about me, and laughing? And then Walter sent me here, to let me rot in this pile of rocks, while the stench of the enemy washes down upon me day and night! *Do you know what that was like?*" His hand strayed to the hilt of the poisoned knife, and for a moment Bert thought he would draw it. But his uncle just growled and turned away. With trembling hands he ladled the poison from the cauldron into a bucket. "No time to talk now!" Uncle Hugh said. "There are arrows to treat and a baron to greet!" He carried the bucket up the Tunnel of Stars, leaving behind the dying echoes of his eerie laugh.

Bert covered his face with his hands and rolled onto his side. *Oh Father*, he thought. *This is all my fault. I am so sorry, so sorry, so sorry.*

And then he heard the voice of the mirror again inside his skull.

It said, *Bertram. Turn your eyes to me.*

Bert shivered so hard that his knees rattled together. When he turned he knew he'd see the slithering face of worms again. It wanted to feed one more time. Maybe for the last time.

CHAPTER

44

Will was flat on his stomach with just the top of his head raised above the lip of the ravine where they hid. The moon was still high among the stars, casting silvery light over the landscape. He saw The Crags before them with rugged black peaks at its back. Beyond the mountains the sky blushed pink before the rising sun. To the south was the road where the baron would thunder along at any minute. To the north was the open ground they needed to cross unseen—a narrow plain littered with shrubs, boulders that had bounded down from the mountains eons before, and the blackened remains of a village.

Parley crawled up the embankment next to Will and patted his back. "I wish we left you somewhere safe," the courier said. "You've been through enough."

"No choice, remember?" Will said, tapping the amulet.

"Humph," Parley said. "You can't fool me. You *want* to be here. I can see it in your eyes. You finally broke through your shell, lad. And it doesn't surprise me a bit that there was a mighty eagle inside all along."

Something caught Parley's attention, and he looked down to see Mokh tugging at his pant leg. The molton thumped its chest with its hand, made a long show of mysterious gestures, and finally held out its stone paw to Parley. The courier shook it.

"What was that about, little friend? I have no idea," Parley said.

Harth had seen it. He hesitated before speaking. "The molton tells you to be careful, Par Lee. It likes you, but . . . fears that it will not see you again after this."

Parley grinned and rapped Mokh on the head with his knuckles. "What a funny chunk of stone you are, Mokh. What, have you had a premonition? I'll be fine, you'll see." Will looked at Harth in time to see him exchange a frown with Kholl and a slow shake of their shaggy heads. He was about to crawl over to the elder Dwergh and ask him what it meant when Andreas spoke.

"Something is strange about this."

"What?" said Harth.

Andreas pointed to The Crags. "They just threw the gate wide open. A minute ago, the walls were full of men—too many, if you ask me. Now I can't see one. And look at that handful of soldiers outside the open gate. They look like they're waiting for something, don't they?"

"Well, they *are* waiting for something," Parley said. "The mirror would know that the baron is coming, wouldn't it?"

"Yes, yes," said Andreas, pounding the lip of the embankment with his fist. "Then why so few? And why open the gate at all?"

Will pressed his fingers against his temples. *Bert, why are you doing this?* "They *want* my father to ride in," he said.

"Yes. It's a trap. And a clever one, considering your father's reputation," Andreas said. "Let's hope he follows the plan."

"We shall know soon enough," Harth said, jutting his chin southward.

A mile down the road, where it turned and ran straight for The Crags, Will saw flickering points of light appear. They were torches held high by a hundred riders. The hoof beats came like thunder before a storm.

"All of you—with me!" said Kholl, and he crawled over the embankment, rose to his feet, and ran as quickly as his short, thick legs could carry him. Andreas pushed Will ahead of him and followed, and Parley and the rest of the Dwergh came behind with Mokh at the rear.

They ran, following gullies and cracks in the plain whenever they could, and shielding themselves behind boulders and charred buildings. Will and Andreas paused behind the black skeleton of a cottage and waited for Parley to catch up. The baron and his riders drew closer and closer with torches bobbing. Will saw the men in front of The Crags point with exaggerated surprise at the charge. They leaped up and down, clutched their heads, and ran pell-mell through the open gate. Will was sure he heard his father shout something in response. The hoof beats quickened.

"Don't do it, Baron," Andreas muttered. Parley finally reached them, and they ran together toward the ledge.

Kholl had already reached the slope of rock that would conceal them from nearly all of the watchtowers of The Crags, and he turned and waved to the rest, urging them to hurry. When Will arrived, he leaned out again to see what would happen. He sensed Andreas peering over his shoulder.

The gate was still wide open, though a man on the wall above it waved his arms madly and shouted for it to be shut. *Brocuff*, Will thought grimly, recognizing the booming voice. The gate didn't move an inch. On the road, just a hundred yards away, Will recognized his father by the light of his torch, leading the charge.

Will's throat went dry. The baron's riders kept coming closer to the gate, churning the dirt of the road. It was strangely quiet on the walls of The Crags—not a soul was in sight.

"Father, please," he whispered. "Stop. *Stop!*"

The baron pulled back on his reins and called for the riders to halt.

There was a commotion within The Crags: angry shouts, running steps, and clattering weapons. An army of archers appeared at the top of the wall. The baron's men spun their horses and retreated. Arrows flitted across the night sky, catching slivers of moonlight. But the riders were beyond reach, and the arrows clattered harmlessly on the ground.

Will was suddenly aware that he hadn't taken a breath for what seemed like an hour. He filled his chest with warm night air and let it out through a smile. "Come on," Andreas said into his ear. "Somewhere the general of the east is smiling. Now your father will keep his distance, call out rude threats, and hold their attention as long as possible. Let us do our part as well as he's done his."

Kortz had already ventured onto the northern ledge, a rocky slope that melded into the steep mountainside. It was a havoc of rocks and rubble, with a thousand shadowy holes and crevices. Beyond that was the swampy lake that cut off any hope of escape should they be seen.

"Oh me. How are we supposed to find the passage in all this?" Parley said, scratching the back of his head. "Do you suppose the Dwergh have better eyes in the dark than us?"

Kortz pulled something from his pocket—a piece of inscribed metal, shaped like a tear drop, at the end of a delicate chain. *A plumb*, Will thought. Kortz let it dangle perfectly still, and watched it carefully. Will stepped closer, wondering what it was for. The plumb began to swing back and forth, and Will was sure he saw it pause unnaturally at one end of its swing as if some invisible force held it briefly. Kortz seemed to agree. He pocketed the thing and moved in that direction, scrambling over rugged stones.

"Some Dwergh magic, you suppose?" Parley said into Will's ear. Will shrugged. They hid behind an outcropping of rock while Kortz led the search. Will leaned out to look back at The Crags. Most of it was hidden, but there was a lone watchtower that jutted beyond the sloping mountainside. He didn't see anyone in the tower, and hoped it stayed that way. The sky behind the mountain grew brighter, and the dimmest stars began to vanish. "We don't have much time," Will said.

"Come—we should stay closer to Kortz," Andreas said. They moved from their hiding place and headed for where Kortz and the others crawled over the ledge, peering into crevices. Will turned to look back at The Crags again. This time he saw the inky shape of a watchman in the tower. The silhouette was in profile, eyeing the road where the baron and his men still lingered. But then his head turned. Will saw him lean out toward the northern ledge, freeze for a moment, and then bolt from the watchtower. Andreas cursed under his breath as the watchman's distant shout drifted toward them.

"We've been seen," Will said.

Kholl grunted. He shouted to Kortz, who only threw up his hands and consulted his plumb again. All the Dwergh scrambled like frenzied ants over the rocks. Mokh hopped from boulder to boulder, diving into smaller spaces and crawling out.

"They can't find it!" Parley said. "A change of plans may be in order, boys. Perhaps retreat?"

"We *have* to find it!" Will cried. Already he heard distant footsteps and metallic clangs—the sound of a small army issuing from the gates of The Crags and coming their way. Will joined the search, sticking his head into a promising gap between the rocks. *Nothing!* He lifted his head to look for another place to explore, and a fluttering sound passed his ear.

Bats. The sun was about to peek over the spine of the mountain. Night was ending. Will watched the small jagged shapes—dozens of them—spiral madly across the sky and converge. On a steep part of the ledge not far away, they vanished into a narrow, nearly invisible crack.

Will shouted. "Hey! *Look at the bats!*"

There was a moment of hesitation, and then the Dwergh raced as one for the spot. Mokh scurried after them. Will and Parley and Andreas followed. The crack led to a narrow corridor inside the ledge. The knight was the last to slip through the slender entrance. "Those men hadn't gotten around the bend yet," he said. "We won't be followed immediately. Is this it, Kholl?"

It was too dark to see, but Will heard Kholl answer. "It almost certainly is."

"Then let us smash this mirror," said Andreas. "And save the boy from its spell if we can. But be careful—if those beasts were part of this sorcery, we will probably meet them again."

CHAPTER

45

It seemed to Bert that his body was like the shed skin of a snake: a paper shell that only mimicked its former self with nothing inside. The wormy horror had fed on him a second time. He knew he wouldn't survive a third feeding.

The first time the thing in the mirror drew out that misty, sparkly stuff—he had to believe it was his very soul—all the colors he saw faded to the subtlest hues. Now everything was without color at all. It was the same ghostly gray wherever he gazed, as if the world died with him. Only the mirror retained its dazzling beauty. It still glimmered with radiant light, while the voracious thing inside had sunk back into the depths to digest its meal.

The thing in the mirror took my soul, Bert thought. *And my laughter. And my love. And my dreams. And my hope.*

He wondered if it devoured the last scrap of his sanity as well. Because he was surely seeing things. Past the dozing beasts and the box where Aunt Elaine was encased, where the passage to the outside lay, something absurd poked its head into the chamber, and then crept in. It was a little stone creature, knee-high, that walked on two legs like a man. Bert raised his head off the floor to stare at it. He closed his eyes and opened them again, expecting the vision to disappear, but the creature was still there. It looked around with glittering eyes, fixed its gaze on the mirror and the beasts, and then slipped back into the passage.

I've gone mad, Bert thought. A moment later more silent figures emerged: Short but powerful men with long thick beards, holding broad axes. No, they weren't men. *Dwergh!* Bert would have been alarmed, but he knew they couldn't be real. He counted them. *Seven, of course.* He would have laughed if there was any humor left inside him.

The Dwergh moved forward with uncanny stealth. Their eyes were dark and fierce, and they were heavily armored with plates on their chests and wide, metal bands around their forearms. One looked older than the rest. He pointed at the pack of dozing beasts sprawled on the chamber floor, surrounding the mirror.

Then Bert saw something that might have made him shout in surprise if he'd had the strength or the spirit: His old friend Parley followed the Dwergh out of the passage. And then came the most incredible apparition of all.

Will?

Is it really you? And who's that with you . . . is that your knight?

It was an eerie moment, surely a dream, with all of

them creeping softly toward the mirror. And then, as they passed the box that held his aunt, Bert heard her voice cleave the silence: "Is someone there? Help me—please, let me out!"

A brutal tempest was unleashed. The mirror cried out with a rising clangor. One sleeping beast awoke and leaped up and bellowed its savage cry: "*Death!*" The others scrabbled to their feet, claws raking the stone, and formed a fearsome barrier before the mirror, with foam gushing out of their gnashing jaws. Bert saw the old Dwergh swing his huge ax as easily as a toy, and smash the latch that held shut Aunt Elaine's prison. The lid opened, and she slipped weakly out onto her side.

Uncle Hugh arrived at that same instant—he must have realized somehow that something was wrong. He rushed from the Tunnel of Stars with his broad sword held high, screaming like a barbarian. While his snapping beasts warded off the intruders, he set himself in front of the mirror and shielded its glass with his body.

The beasts attacked, and the Dwergh stood their ground. Bert heard the smash of metal on bone, low cries of pain, animal sounds of anguish. A beast had its jaws clamped on the arm of a Dwergh, but the band of metal kept its teeth from piercing through. The knight was everywhere, hacking and thrusting with his sword wherever one of the beasts had gotten the best of the Dwergh.

Bert heard Will shout. "Look, Parley! Bert's a prisoner! Bert, are you all right?" Bert raised a hand. He felt a tear run down his face. Or was it only a drop of water from the stony ceiling?

A beast with wide, curving horns on its face charged at Will. The knight arrived too late to help. Will seized the horns and pushed away from the clashing jaws. The creature lowered its head, hooked its long horns under Will's legs, and tossed him. Will hurtled through the air, hit the ground, and rolled across a dusty pile of bones near where Aunt Elaine was slumped on the ground, away from the fray. Before the beast could attack again, the knight thrust his sword deep into its side, finding a soft place between the thick plates of bone. The beast roared and thrashed about, taking with it the sword and leaving the knight without a weapon.

Closer to the mirror a gap appeared amid the confusion. Parley hobbled through with his teeth clenched and a sword held tight in his good hand. Only Hugh Charmaigne stood between him and the mirror.

"Out of my way, Lord Charmaigne," Parley cried. "We have to smash it!"

Uncle Hugh laughed. Bert would have covered his eyes if he had the strength—anyone could see that the lame courier was no match for Lord Charmaigne, the seasoned fighter. Parley raised his sword as Uncle Hugh swung his. The clash of metal was harsh, and Parley's sword was driven to the ground. With his other hand,

Uncle Hugh pulled the knife out of its sheath. Parley saw it coming, and curved his body to avoid the slashing arc. Bert saw the fabric of Parley's shirt tear across his stomach, and the courier fell onto his back.

The little stone creature darted out from the chaos and raced for the mirror. Uncle Hugh saw it and raised his sword. But before he could strike, one of the beasts leaped at it from behind, seized its legs in its jaws, and dashed it on the hard floor. The stone creature shattered. Its legs and arms tumbled away amid a cloud of ash and sparks. Parley screamed something; it sounded like "mock."

Bert watched the little stone head roll across the floor and bump into his leg. He reached down and picked it up. It fit easily in his hand, this strange skull with diamonds for eyes. As he watched, the gems twinkled with inner light and went dark.

Bert didn't know what the stone creature was, but he knew what it just tried to do. What they were all risking their lives for—his brother, the men, and the Dwergh. It was what had to be done.

The beasts were winning their battle. Two of the Dwergh were wounded, and some had lost their weapons. Uncle Hugh laughed and screamed at the same time. "Kill them! All of them!" He stepped forward. Behind him Bert could see the mirror, shimmering with cold light.

When he saw it again, Bert realized that the mirror

hadn't sapped his every feeling. Fury remained. It gave him a final trickle of strength. Bert pushed himself to his knees. The air was thick as mud. He lifted one knee and put his foot flat on the floor. The chain around his leg weighed a thousand pounds. The world tilted and heaved, and dark spots dimmed his vision. He got his other foot under him, and rose unsteadily.

When he lifted the stone head and brought it back behind his ear, he lurched and nearly fell. He took a deep breath and looked toward the mirror again. He paused, trying to gather strength. And yet . . . part of him didn't want to do it. Part of him still wanted the mirror back—hoped that it could be his once more. The hunk of stone began to slip from his hand. And then he thought of his brother.

With every last bit of strength he possessed, Bert hurled the stone head, falling as he flung it. The rock soared in a graceful curve through the dark air, slowly turning. Uncle Hugh saw it from the corner of his eye, but not in time. The head struck the mirror, just below the top of the frame, and Bert was sure that the diamond eyes had touched it first.

Uncle Hugh cried out in pain. He dropped his sword and clapped a hand across his face. Bert felt a stab of pain too, as if a blade had pierced his skull. The world flickered and blurred. When he could focus again, he saw Uncle Hugh in front of the mirror. He'd dropped his knife and sword, and pressed his palms against the glass.

"No," Uncle Hugh cried. "Don't! Don't break! *You can't break!*"

On either side of his uncle's hands, Bert saw jagged lines spreading. There were sharp cracking noises, like ice melting in water. *Tik tik tik.* A new sound arose from the mirror—a high shriek unlike anything Bert had ever heard, growing stronger and shriller by the second. It was too painful to bear. The fighting stopped, and people and Dwergh alike covered their ears. The beasts twisted their heads to and fro, as if the sound could be shaken off, and then they dashed out of the chamber except for a pair that lay dead on the ground.

Even through the unearthly howl and past the thumbs jammed into his ears, Bert heard the splintering cracks of the mirror. *TIK! TIK! TIK!* Uncle Hugh staggered back from the glass. The worm face was there for Bert's uncle to see at last, its mouth open and screaming, and all its bulbous eyes staring out between the wriggling masses. The cracked surface bulged outward, distorting the face even more.

The old Dwergh shouted. Bert couldn't catch the words, but he saw what the others did. They dropped to the ground and covered their heads with their arms. Some dove behind the fallen beasts. Aunt Elaine and Will crawled behind the cauldron. Bert curled his body into a ball and put his back to the mirror. He thought he might be screaming himself, but he wasn't sure. He couldn't hear it if he was.

One day, years before, Bert and Will were in their favorite hideaway—the abandoned watchtower. They foolishly stayed to watch as a fierce thunderstorm swept over Ambercrest, and lightning struck so close that the clap of thunder arrived in the same instant. They saw a jagged column of white fire and smelled burning air. The sound rattled their bones and stabbed at their ears.

Now, here in the secret chamber under The Crags, when the mirror shattered, it made that bolt seem dim as a firefly and the sound as soft as snapping fingers.

The light of the explosion scorched Bert's eyes, though he'd turned away and shut them. The blast rang in his brain, like a gong. A wave of air hurled him back with the chain dragging behind him, and he slammed into the wall. He heard pieces of glass shatter on stone, and felt icy slashes of pain across his legs and his back.

He had to remind himself to breathe again. Was it completely dark? No, he'd just forgotten to open his eyes. He opened them. Beside him, on the ground, he saw a bat lying on its back, twitching as it came to its senses. It turned over sluggishly and launched into a weak and awkward flight. Bert watched it flap past the knight, the first on his feet.

The knight walked unsteadily toward the cauldron, waving at the dust that hung in the air. The Dwergh lifted their shaggy heads and peered toward the mirror.

Bert followed their gaze. He raised his arm to block the sight of his uncle's ruined body. Uncle Hugh was no more; a glimpse told him that. He sensed, in a strange, detached way, that he should feel something. Sorrow. Pity. Relief. *Something.* But he only knew that he didn't want to see what the flying shards had done to his uncle when the mirror shattered.

Only a few jagged pieces remained in the frame. Bert squinted and blinked. Behind where the glass once stood, there was . . . *a deep, black space.* It didn't make sense to his eye. There shouldn't have been any depth there. He should have seen the far side of the chamber through the empty frame. But instead there was a dark void, and looming inside it, that awful face. It bobbed weakly on its jointed neck. Worms dribbled off like beads of sweat and splattered on the stone floor. The head sagged onto the spikes of glass on the bottom of the frame, and whatever force held it together withered and failed. The wriggling things spilled onto the floor of the chamber, sweeping the bobbing, senseless eyes with them, and it all dissolved into a noxious, steaming, gray puddle.

Bert heard Will call his name. His brother hopped

toward him, keeping an injured foot off the ground. He kneeled and clutched Bert's hand. There was a smile on Will's face at first, but then his expression went grim. Bert could hear his voice dimly. "Bert—what is it? Are you all right?"

Bert stared up blankly. How could he explain what the mirror had stolen from him—that most of him was gone, and he was only a husk of the person he used to be, an egg with no white or yolk inside. He couldn't bear to look into Will's eyes, so he stared past his brother. And he saw something come out from the void, and drift across the chamber as if carried by a breeze. It looked like the smoke from a snuffed candle, but it was pure white and filled with the tiniest, twinkling lights.

I've seen that before, Bert thought. It was a struggle even to think; his mind was muddled. He tried to remember when. *Of course. When it left me.*

Will gasped as the mist snaked over his shoulder and drifted toward Bert. "Don't," Bert said in a whisper as Will tried to fan it away. "Leave it be!" He watched the mist touch his hands and chest, where beads of dry blood still dotted his skin. The mist pooled for a moment, and then seeped inside. A little tail of white was the last thing to vanish.

Will stared, openmouthed. "Bert, what is that?"

"It's . . . me," Bert whispered. The other tendrils soaked into him. Bert felt a change inside—a rain after weeks of drought, a meal after famine, a ray of sun after endless night. His heart bounded. It was coming back. *He* was coming back. He grabbed Will's hand and squeezed it. "It's me!" He found that he could rise, and he got up on his knees and wrapped his arms weakly around his brother. Color seeped back into the world. When he glimpsed his uncle's body again, there was pain in his heart.

He saw Parley sitting up, not far from the mirror. The courier had the little stone head in his hands, cradling it against his chest. One of the Dwergh came to him and put a hand on his shoulder.

A Dwergh shouted something and pointed at the shattered mirror. They all looked, and gasped as one.

A spectral form emerged from the void. It was a long-bearded Dwergh with a silver crown, wearing a robe and holding a staff. He hovered before the mirror, and Bert was sure that he looked with interest at the Dwergh next to Parley who bowed his head. All the Dwergh did the same, and some of them covered their hearts with their hands as well. The ghostly shape nodded. He shuddered, and then he rose and vanished like smoke from a fire, gone before he touched the stony ceiling of the chamber.

More figures emerged, pale and gauzy. They looked like Dwergh lords of old. Each of them paused to look about, and Bert was sure he saw something in their eyes—a deep satisfaction, an infinite relief—before they too flew up and disappeared.

It was only when Parley fell onto his side that Bert's attention was torn away from the sight of the spirits.

"Par Lee, what is wrong?" said the Dwergh by his side.

"Don't know, Harth," said Parley. He looked confused. His face was an odd, sickly color, and slick with sweat. "I got away without a scratch—almost." He lifted his torn shirt with the hand that wasn't holding the stone creature's head. Bert's heart sank when he saw the red line traced across Parley's belly.

"No," Bert said, releasing his brother from the embrace. "Please, no . . ."

"What, Bert?" said Will.

"Uncle's knife. It was poisoned!"

"Poisoned? Oh me," Parley said weakly. He looked down at the little stone head. "You were right, little friend. You and I . . . won't see each other . . . again." The stone rolled out of his grasp onto the floor.

Bert splayed his fingers across his eyes. *Not Parley*, he thought. *Not Parley.*

Between his fingers he saw another ghostly form emerge from the mirror. This was no Dwergh. He recognized her immediately. He struggled to his feet. Will helped him with an arm wrapped around his waist.

"Rohesia!" Bert cried. "Don't leave yet! You can help him!"

Everyone in the chamber was perfectly still: Will, the

seven Dwergh, the knight, and Aunt Elaine, who was leaning on the cauldron. They all stared at the ghost of the Witch-Queen, as beautiful now as she'd been in life, as beautiful as she'd been in the portrait Bert saw in what seemed like another age. At first she didn't seem to hear the plea as she drifted before the shattered mirror. But her head turned slowly, and Bert looked into her pale eyes. He pointed. "Help him! The poison will kill him!" The lovely specter drifted toward Parley with her ghostly dress billowing. The courier's sweaty face was contorted with pain, but still he gawked up at her, entranced.

Rohesia raised one hand, palm up. A breeze swept through the chamber. Near the cauldron, the scattered sheets of parchment ruffled, and a single piece of paper fluttered high and came down again. Aunt Elaine snatched it from the dusty air and stared, wide-eyed. "This is her writing," she said. She looked at Rohesia. "*Your* writing."

The specter smiled. She gestured again, and Bert heard a clatter from the shelves that held the ancient jars and bottles. One of the jars tipped over and rolled forward. Aunt Elaine limped over and picked it up. She read the script on its side, and ran toward Parley as fast as she could. Andreas took her arm and helped her along.

Rohesia closed her eyes, and Bert was sure he heard

a deep, happy sigh fill the chamber. The specter rose and faded. A moment later the Witch-Queen was gone. When Bert looked at the mirror again, it was only an empty frame. The void had vanished.

CHAPTER

47

"Mother, please," Bert cried, laughing. "You and Father are driving me crazy. I can walk perfectly well!"

"Honestly, Bert," the baroness said. "Why can't you just use the cane for another week until you've gotten all your strength back? You'll fall and break your neck, and where will that leave me? After I almost lost you once—almost lost both of you . . ." She chewed on the back of a finger.

Bert put an arm around her shoulder and kissed her cheek. "We're fine now."

"All of this . . . It was all my fault," the baroness said. "Sending you here."

"No more of that, Mother. Everything's fine now."

She sniffed and wiped a tear with the back of her hand. "It will be fine when we all get back to Ambercrest. This place frightens me. It always has."

"It shouldn't scare you anymore," Bert said. "The trouble is over. But I'm looking forward to getting home too. And then preparing for the next journey, when I'm really strong enough."

The baroness put a hand on his cheek. "Are you sure you want to do that?"

Bert squeezed her hand. "Oh yes. Why don't you make sure all your things are packed, Mother? I'll talk to you later."

When she'd left, Bert leaned out on the wall of the terrace and breathed deeply. He heard footsteps behind him. The rhythm was familiar: a strong step, then a weak step.

"Good morning, Parley," he said without turning around.

"Speak up, will you? Don't forget, I'm deaf in one ear now," Parley said.

The courier leaned on the balcony. Bert looked at him. "You look even happier than usual today."

Parley grinned and rubbed his stomach. "Makes me giddy just to be alive, Bert. Besides, how many men can say they were saved by the world's loveliest ghost?" He sighed and put a hand into the pocket of his vest. Bert knew what was in there: a pair of diamonds that Parley would keep with him for the rest of his life. Parley looked at him sideways. "It was a month ago today, did you know that?"

"Yes."

"You know which bit I wish I'd seen? When those beasts ran into the courtyard and scared the stuffing out of Brocuff and the rest of those knaves."

Bert laughed. "At least poor Uncle's poison arrows were good for something."

"Yes. Funny how it all worked out. Seeing those

monsters convinced your uncle's men that maybe they hadn't signed up on the right side after all."

Bert nodded. He turned to look at the mountains of the Dwergh, looming behind The Crags. He lost himself in his thoughts until he heard Parley speak again.

"And there's something else that may eventually work out, if I'm not mistaken," the courier said. He pointed into the courtyard below, where Aunt Elaine and Andreas walked side by side. The knight staggered under the weight of an enormous potted plant while Aunt Elaine pointed to its leaves and lectured with great enthusiasm about its medicinal powers.

"What do you mean?" Bert said.

Parley clapped a hand on his forehead. "How is it that the fellow with one eye sees twice as much as the rest of you?"

"Oh. *Oh!*" Bert laughed until he had to wipe his eyes. Then he told Parley something that only his mother and father knew. "Last night I told my father that when the time comes, Will should be baron. I said I don't want it to be me."

Parley stared at him. "Did you really?"

Bert shrugged. "I . . . lost my taste for it. For power. Fighting. Ruling. All that. You know, I'm sure Will's going to be better at all those things." He reached into his pocket and pulled out the little sachet of melissa that Aunt Elaine had made for him. He brought it to his nose and took a deep whiff. "There's something else I'd like to do with my life, I think."

"What's that?" Parley asked.

"I'll tell you," Bert said. "And by the way, I was wondering if you'd like to join me."

CHAPTER

48

Margaret leaned close to Will and pinched his waist. "Calm down, boy!" whispered his old friend and servant.

"I can't help it," Will shot back from the side of his mouth. He bounced up and down again, as if there were springs on his heels.

The courtyard at Ambercrest was lined with knights, soldiers, and nobles from throughout the kingdom. The king himself stood beside Baron Charmaigne.

On the wall above the gates heralds lifted their trumpets and blasted long, clear notes that echoed off the keep. Cheers drifted over the wall from outside, where thousands crowded the roadside.

The gates of Ambercrest were thrown open, and Will nearly shouted aloud as three figures on horseback rode in. One was the king's ambassador. The one in the middle had to be Tarkho, highest of the seven kings of the Dwergh. And the other was Bert. *He looks so much bigger,* Will thought. *I suppose I do too.*

Familiar folk rode in next: Kholl and Harth and the rest of the band of seven, adorned with so much shining silver and gold it was a wonder their horses didn't buckle under the weight. Parley was with them, trying at first to look grave and important, but soon surrendering his face to a radiant grin.

For the first time in nearly a century there was peace again between this kingdom and the Dwergh. Will gazed at his brother, and his heart warmed. He saw Bert look back at him. Bert winked, and pointed with a subtle finger toward their favorite hideaway, the old watchtower, before turning and saying something to the Dwergh king. Tarkho nodded.

My brother, Will thought. *The peacemaker.*

What a mighty thing to be.